TRUTH SERUM PRESS

STORIES

MY
GAY
UNCLE
TOLD
ME

TRUTH SERUM
VOL. 3

First published as a collection August 2019
Content copyright © Truth Serum Press and individual authors
Edited by Matt Potter

BP#00080

Truth Serum Press
32 Meredith Street
Sefton Park SA 5083
Australia

Email: truthserumpress@live.com.au
Website: https://truthserumpress.net/
Store: https://truthserumpress.net/catalogue/

Original cover image copyright © Ryan McGuire
Cover design copyright © Matt Potter

ISBN: 978-1-925536-86-7

Also available as an eBook
ISBN: 978-1-925536-87-4

A note on differences in punctuation and spelling

Truth Serum Press proudly features writers from all over the English-speaking world.
Some speak and write English as their first language, while for others, it's their
second or third or even fourth language. Naturally, across all versions of English,
there are differences in punctuation and spelling, and even in meaning. These
differences are reflected in the work *Truth Serum Press* publishes, and they account for
any differences in punctuation, spelling and meaning found within these pages.

Truth Serum Press is a member of the
Bequem Publishing collective
http://www.bequempublishing.com/

RUBINA

ALEX REECE ABBOTT

SARA ABEND-SIMS

HENRY BLADON

STEVE BOGDANIEC

STEVE CARR

HELEN CHAMBERS

CARL CHAPMAN

CHUKA SUSAN CHESNEY

CAROLYN CORDON

RUTH Z. DEMING

EG DOWNS

TOM FEGAN

NOD GHOSH

JAN HAAG

CHRIS HALL

ALISDAIR HODGSON

EDDY KNIGHT

LANCE MANION

COLLEEN MOYNE

EDWARD O'DWYER

DELEON W. PEACOCK

MATT POTTER

MELISA QUIGLEY

MICHELE SAINT-YVES

E.M. STORMO

SUSAN WHITMORE

This book is,
rather predictably,
dedicated to
every fabulous
gay uncle out there

and also those
gay uncles
who,
while perhaps not
being quite so fabulous

certainly show
there might
be another way
of doing and thinking
and being
and seeing ...

Jennie Kincaid

Jan Haag

My father used to say that Jennie Kincaid walked like a boy, but what would you expect from the only girl in a family with three boys and a dad who owned a motorcycle shop? Jennie was my sister's best friend, and my father, a master of all things mechanical, admired Jennie's willingness to "get her hands dirty." So did my sister, though I was happier reading a book.

My father's comment was meant admiringly. He liked women who could "handle themselves," as he said. When Jennie came over, my dad liked to have some kind of mechanical project going. She had to pass through the garage to get in our house, and Dad would snag her before she hit the door, saying, "You need to see what I've got on the workbench." And Jennie would ooh and ahh over the carburetor my father had torn apart or bicycle parts he was reassembling. My sister would join them, and they'd spend hours in the garage (in bad weather) or on the patio (in good weather) with parts and tools and grease spread all over sheets of newspaper.

My father was in heaven handing wrenches to the girls ("try this seven-eighths") or putting new spark plugs on the lawn mower. I'd wander outside to see them kneeling on the ground, heads together, discussing this doo-hickey or that thing-a-ma-jig that had gone all catty-wampus. At the end of an afternoon they'd come inside to wash their filthy hands.

"You should've been a shop teacher," my mother told my father.

"Nah," my father would say. "I wouldn't want to deal with a bunch of boys."

Smart, capable girls who didn't mind getting sweaty or dirty made his day.

My dad and the girls were at the workbench the day Uncle Chris showed up in his '65 Ford pickup. He'd driven 12 hours straight from Idaho Falls to us in Eugene.

"What've you got here?" he said to my dad. "Hey, Carla," he greeted my sister.

"Hey, Uncle Chris," my sister responded. "This is my friend Jennie. We're adjusting sprinkler heads." Jennie held up a weird-looking, key-shaped tool.

Uncle Chris didn't know a torque wrench from a screw-driver. "Uh huh," he said but hung around to watch the fix-it crew.

When he came in the house, I was tucked into an alcove in the stairwell, a great vantage point for overhearing grownup discussions.

"Helen," Uncle Chris said to my mother. "I gotta talk to you."

He lowered his voice, but I caught the phrase "something different about Jennie."

"I'm pretty sure she likes girls," he said.

"Well, of *course*, she does. She's a girl."

Silence from Uncle Chris. "Helen, I think she's gonna be one of those women who… you know."

"I don't know, Chris. What on earth are you talking about?" Mom leveled her don't-mess-with-me voice at her brother.

More silence. Then, "I think she's gonna be a lesbian, Helen, and you might want to know that. Since she's Carla's best friend and all."

That stopped Mom. "How would you know?"

"I know," Chris's voice hit his shoes. "Trust me. I know."

I peeled myself from the alcove and headed to my father's office where he kept a seldom-used Webster's to look up "lesbian." When I found it, my eyebrows hit my hairline.

A couple of days later Carla said, "Do you know what a lesbian is?"

"Of course," I said, wondering who'd dropped that word into her ear.

"Do you think Jennie's one?" Her blue eyes blinked fast.

"No," I said, having no idea, "but so what? She's great. We all like her."

Carla said nothing, but in the months that followed, she saw Jennie less frequently. By the time the girls entered high school in 1972, the only time they spent together was in band, Jennie playing French horn and Carla playing clarinet, me banging on tympani, though we all remained friendly.

Dad continued to encourage Jennie, and when she was 16, he helped her get a job in a parts warehouse. After a couple of weeks on the job, Jennie invited Dad to visit her at work, where he heard two men call Jennie "a bad word," my father told my mother.

"What word?" my mother asked.

"They called her," Dad lowered his voice, "a *dyke*. I told them that was a terrible thing to say. Jennie just likes doing mechanical things. And she's good at 'em, too."

The next time Uncle Chris visited, my mother relayed this news as I eavesdropped. "I'm not surprised," he said.

Later, Carla and I found Uncle Chris out by his pickup. "Hey, Uncle Chris, can we ask you a question?" I called.

His teeth gleamed against his sunburned face. "Sure, hon. What's up?"

I told him what I'd heard.

"Yeah," Carla said. "What's the big deal? She's our friend."

I nodded in sister solidarity.

Uncle Chris leaned against the truck. "It's not a big deal. Really. No matter what some people think. Some girls like girls, and some boys like boys." He looked into our widening eyes. "You know, for girlfriends or boyfriends."

His eyes narrowed. "And if you hear people calling those kids 'dykes' or 'fags', you tell 'em to shut up." He ran a hand over his forehead. "You be nice to those kids. Be their friend. Don't make fun of 'em, you understand?"

We nodded.

"Good," he said. "Everybody needs someone to love 'em. You remember that love shows up for folks in different ways. OK?"

We nodded again.

I was in my 20s before I realized that Uncle Chris came out to us that day. We never spoke of it again, and he remained single—as far as we knew—for the rest of his life.

Jennie, however, did find a very nice girlfriend with whom she started a roofing business. Years later they re-shingled my parents' house.

My father stood on the lawn for days watching them work. He was so proud.

Butter

EG Downs

He used to eat butter like it was candy. That's what Derek and Mom would always tell me, whenever I would liberally apply butter to my toast, or my grits, or to my already buttered potatoes. He would grab a stick of cold butter from the fridge and gnaw at it gently, he would apply room temperature butter to gingersnap cookies, he would dip carrots in butter.

"We joke that he was more likely to be your father than your father was," Uncle Derek told me. "You have his eyes, somehow, and you do have his love for butter." But he was dead years before I was born.

They used to tell me this story all the time, like it meant anything to me. They had lots of friends who had died before I was born, overdoses and AIDS mostly, but a few tragic accidents. I guess that was what it was like to live fast and young, something they would never let me do.

But they always talked about him. There was something special about him, and it wasn't just his love for butter. One early evening, the back and forth story-telling routine began, triggered as usual by my request for more butter.

"He was gorgeous," my mom would say.

"GORGEOUS!" Derek would scream.

They didn't tell me stories about him because I asked, or even listened that much, but to remind themselves of what he was like. To hear each other, to remember him.

"He was gorgeous and he didn't know it," Derek would go on. "Which always makes someone extra cute. And he was so sweet. Soft-spoken and polite, but he could be so mischievous! None like him."

"No one was like him!" Mom would interject. "You know, I should have hated Derek for stealing my boyfriend," she would say. "But he was just too good not to share," she would turn from me and look at Derek.

"Wish we hadn't had to share him with that dancer."

They each grew quiet, and one of them would reach for the other's hand, and before the tears came, they would sigh together.

"We were so young!" Derek would laugh.

It was their routine, I nodded along while I finished my food. I knew he was special, but I was so young. I didn't know what it was like to lose your love, your shared love, with only the same few stories to preserve his memory. But when Mom got up to get dessert, Derek started to trail off, a new story I hadn't heard, a break from the routine.

"I remember one time, we were tripping, acid was such a thing then. And we decided to go for a swim. The water was so calm that day, even though the sun was starting to set, our high minds just told us to jump right in! We floated, staring at the sky, hallucinating and giggling. We were naked!" he said, remembering the details as he spoke.

I put my fork down, I was listening then.

"It was getting darker, and we were probably peaking. We couldn't see the shore. I remember starting to panic, for sure we were going to be swept out into the middle of the Atlantic and drown, or get eaten by something! But he was calm, as always. We saw some sort of light and decided to swim toward it, but because we were tripping, our eyes played so many tricks on us. I would get distracted and follow the reflections of the sky on the water, but he still had a strong sense of direction. We swam and swam and then we saw the boat. We screamed and waved it over and an old, scruffy fisherman was driving it. I remember him looking at us skeptically, we were so young and skinny and naked! But the fisherman let us hop on, gave us towels and asked us how we ended up out here, where we needed to go. We were heading back and then he started to question us more. I remember him, the fisherman, muttering something like 'two young men naked in the water... seems weird that's all.' But he was our only ride out of the water! We held each other in fear and because we were cold... and in love. And he saw us and started to yell at us, 'are y'all gay?' again and again! But then we started to laugh, well I did because he did, and then we saw the shore. The fisherman started to slow down and we just jumped out so we didn't have to answer! We were laughing so hard we could barely swim back to shore..." he started to trail off.

The super gay story

Lance Manion

My mother has three brothers. They are all gay. She describes their gayness in terms of the porridge in *Goldilocks and the Three Bears*. It's impossible to tell that one of her brothers is gay. One of the brothers you can tell he's gay but only if you pay attention. The third brother, the one she calls Aunt Steve, is wildly, over-the-top gay. Super gay.

I remember the first time I met my aunt; it was as if he was worried that everyone in the restaurant wouldn't know that they were dining with a gay man in the building. He was wearing a shawl that looked like he stole it from his grandmother and he squealed a lot when he talked. By the time he ordered his meal even the cooks knew there was a gay man in attendance.

Aunt Steve was the best.

One summer I went to stay with him for a few days. He lived on a quiet cul-de-sac, which he told me was a metaphor for his love life. At the time I didn't understand the reference but I do remember he got a very faraway look in his eyes as he said it. His house wasn't anything like I imagined it would be. I expected pink leather sofas and orange shag carpet everywhere.

Instead it looked like every other home I'd ever been in. I was a little deflated and I told him as much.

Then he told me a story about trying to fit in. A story I will retell to my children when they are old enough to understand... and I fully understand it myself.

At one time Aunt Steve did have a pink leather sofa and all of the other garish things I was expecting from my super gay relation. The problem was that none of his neighbors would ever come over to visit because the contents of his super gay house made them uncomfortable.

Even people going door to door to talk about the Lord or selling cookies to raise money for Little League started skipping his house.

Even his two gay brothers apparently had something to say about his décor.

"Want to know what I did?" he asked me one day.

"Of course," I replied.

Apparently, every year everyone in the cul-de-sac would hold a joint garage sale. They would all chip in to publicize it and it became something of a tradition. There were fourteen families taking part that fateful Sunday morning.

"The night before I arranged to have six workers meet at my house at seven in the morning."

My head swam as I listened. What super gay thing could Aunt Steve possibly have planned?

"The garage sale was scheduled to open at seven thirty. At seven twenty nine I strode up the driveway of my closest neighbor and made an offer on all of their stuff."

I can't be entirely sure but I'm guessing my eyes shone as I listened.

"'I'll take it!' I announced to my shocked neighbor. 'I'll pay whatever is on the little sticky tags. Deal?' I asked him."

At this point I'm entirely sure my eyes were glistening. I had no idea where this was going but I loved it.

"He was shocked. He didn't know what to say. My six workers marched up and began bringing the complete contents of his driveway into my house. Furniture, dishes, old board games. You name it."

No one could tell a story like my Aunt Steve.

"I then went to each and every house in the cul-de-sac and bought up their entire offerings. One after another. After a few houses they began to see what was happening and met me on the sidewalk. There was no bartering or squabbling. Fourteen houses in a row. I bought it all. They didn't know what to make of me."

He sat back and smiled at the memory. I looked down at the couch I was sitting on. I looked over to the side table and then across to the kitchen chairs. A light bulb went off.

"That's right, everything you see in here is from my neighbors. I was able to replace everything."

The realization of what he was saying hit me like a ton of bricks. I didn't know how to feel. Was this a story of fitting in or surrendering? He saw the confusion on my face. Sensed I was wrestling with something big.

"Before you ask me if they started to come over and visit more let me finish." There was a little squeal in his voice. "After everything was in my house I had the six workers take out all of my existing stuff and put it on my driveway. I had already priced everything up and it was ready to sell."

I leaned in further, captivated and about to hear the exciting conclusion.

"Let me tell you, it was a feeding frenzy!" Aunt Steve threw up his hands in glee. "I mean, where else could you get a Mauro Oliveira Decorated Chair for fifteen dollars or a Manchester Gay Pride Doodle Map Cushion for fifty cents? The crowds that love garage sales were just showing up and my neighbors no longer had anything to do but take a look. It was pandemonium!"

"Fifteen dollars? Fifty cents?" I thought to myself. I thought this was a story of revenge or at least breaking even. I was feeling a bit crestfallen.

As if answering my unasked question, he continued. "It wasn't about making money. I lost hundreds of dollars that day. Everything I owned was scooped up for pennies on the dollar that day." He paused dramatically. "Just like everyone else."

Slowly a smile crept across my face.

"So it doesn't matter if they come to visit me. I know that my 'Peter Getting out of Nick's Pool' print hangs above the fireplace directly across the street."

Goldilocks be damned, Aunt Steve was just right.

Friendly Relations

Eddy Knight

The first story that my uncle told me was that he wasn't gay. Implied rather than told it I suppose, when my ex- and I paid him a visit once. It came as a surprise as I had always assumed that he was. Not because he was passionate about art, or theatre, or 30s and 40s female movie stars, although he was an absolute devotee of all these. No, the giveaway was that he had been living with Derek for twelve years. House-sharing they called it.

Not that I cared one way or another, gay or straight Raymond was my favourite uncle and nothing could change that. It's just that when you think you know someone, and then suddenly a whole new fact is presented to you, especially one as fundamental as their sexuality, it brings all of your assumptions into question. And, let's face it, our worlds are built more on assumptions than on facts.

It was back in the 70s, I was not long married, and one day driving home from visiting my mother, we called in on the pair of them. Since we still had some distance to travel they offered us a bed for the night.

"It's really no problem," Uncle Raymond said, "It's lovely to see you both, and Derek and I could easily share."

So I decided to check. I mean I'd believed that they'd been 'sharing' for years. On a visit to the upstairs bathroom I stealthily poked my head around both of the bedroom doors. They each had beds but only one was made up with sheets and blankets, only one had ornaments on the chest of drawers, and only one had bedside lamps on either side. It was a relief to have my worldview confirmed. His attempt at misdirection amused me. It was not that long since the law had been repealed and we'd never talked about it. So he didn't know my feelings on the subject, just as he didn't know how much dope I was smoking.

He finally came out to mother and me on the evening of my father's funeral. Amongst the sadness this was a comfort. We were finally able to tell him that we had known for years and that we didn't care.

"What about John?" he asked.

My mother's turn to lie. The subject had never been mentioned, but she told me later that Dad had suspected, and had hated the idea that his younger brother might be a 'poofter'.

"Never occurred to him," she replied, deciding that, like her, he was emotionally overwrought and in tears enough already. We all were. Cleansing tears that forever wiped away all of our secrets and lies, or so I'd thought.

Derek's parents lived in the same town as my mum, so Raymond quite often visited his sister-in-law while Derek fulfilled his family duties. Recently divorced and temporarily without wheels, I had travelled by coach to stay with Mum for a week, at the end of which Raymond turned up for Sunday tea. I hadn't seen him for ages and his good nature coupled with his acerbic wit soon had me laughing out loud, lifting the depression that had weighed me down since the split. He mentioned a production of *The Diary of Anne Frank* he had recently witnessed, in the company of members of a well-known art rock band whose manager was a friend of his. Apparently the performance had been so dire that when the Nazis appeared one of the musicians had shouted out, "She's in the attic."

Seeing me much cheered up, Mum suggested that Raymond could give me a lift back to his place, which would cut in half the time I'd have to spend in the coach. Raymond hesitated for a moment before agreeing. "Yes, why not? Or you could stay the night, we have a spare room, you could travel on in the morning."

Later, in the car, it was confession time again.

"I know your mother says that she doesn't mind…my proclivities, but I don't like to rub her nose in it, as it were. The fact is we're not going straight home. There's a really neat little gay nightclub in town that we've got into the habit of visiting when we're here. So, I could drop you at the coach station now or you could come with us, and back to ours afterwards. You'd be more than welcome."

The town that I'd grown up in was a naval port, which somewhat coloured my reply.

"As long as you guarantee that no burly naval stoker gets me drunk and carries me off, then I'd love to. Gay clubs are supposed to be brilliant."

"I assure you that no harm will befall you. Your eyes might be opened a bit but that's all to the good. If anyone tries to chat you up just tell them that you're with a friend and they'll leave you alone. Unless you want to try, of course…" He left that dangling for a moment before breaking out into raucous laughter.

"No thank you, Uncle Raymond, I think observer status will be more than enough."

We collected Derek, signed in, and it was as brilliant as I had imagined. Colours, flashing lights, dry ice and really pumping music; Prince, Bowie, Pet Shop Boys, and of course the goddess Madonna. A few guys in drag and some in leather but it was a man at the bar wearing a suit who asked me if I wanted to dance. I used the friend line and nodded towards Derek and Raymond thrashing about wildly on the dance floor. Not bad for a couple of middle-aged men, I thought, and before we left I had danced with both of them.

"Well, what did you think?" Raymond asked me as we were leaving.

"It felt like freedom," I replied. "Like a pelican flying."

Grandma and
Steve McQueen

Steve Bogdaniec

You want to hear a good family story? Ugh, are you sure? Did you ever hear the one about the movie *The Getaway?* That's a good one. I think you're old enough now.

Like most good family stories, you're going have to promise to never repeat any of it.

It was 1972. Your grandma wanted Grandpa to stop being a horrible drunk. Grandpa wanted Grandma to stop being a horrible shrew. They were both miserable, on the verge of divorce. The only thing they could agree on was no more kids. Your mom and Uncle Matt were quite enough, thank you.

So what happened? Steve McQueen, the actor, happened. Grandma, Grandpa, and a few of their friends went to a matinee of one of his movies—*The Getaway*—and Grandma fell in love. He was the most dashing, beautiful, dangerous, gorgeous man she had ever seen.

Look him up on your phone. Yep, that's him. Right? I mean, he's ok, but not...well, whatever worked for her.

Mom said she hadn't felt that way in years. Grandma wanted Steve McQueen. You've seen her—she's a grandma.

She's always kind of been that way to me. But she was only 38 in 1972, still a young woman. You don't think 38 is young, but you'll see: it's young. That night, she was still a young woman. Grandma saw Steve McQueen fighting and driving and looking all hot and mean. And rugged. And sexy—ok, I kind of get him. Anyway, he touched her. And then she touched herself—in the dark of the movie theater, sitting there next to her friends and her husband.

I know! Mom told me herself one night when she was drinking. She sounded guilty when she told me, but also kind of turned on at the thought of it too. It was public and private at the same time, in the dark, but still around people, sexy and forbidden. I get that.

But still—what son wants to hear about his mother playing with herself in public? I thought all she was going to talk about was Dad. Mom loves to talk shit about him, especially now that he's gone. I don't get how they were ever together. You remember Grandpa a bit, don't you? He was a little better around the grandkids.

Anyway, your Grandma wanted Steve McQueen, but she couldn't get him. She could *get* Grandpa. So she shuffled Laura and Matt off to someone's house for the night, got into some of Grandpa's bourbon, and proceeded to seduce the hell out of her husband, throwing contraceptives, time of the month, and the fact that she basically despised him to the wind.

I am the result. Loved, certainly, but unplanned, and to a degree, unwanted. Dad didn't need any more pressure to provide, and Mom was pissed that it wasn't Steve McQueen who had knocked her up.

Besides that, Steve McQueen and I bought Mom and Dad another four years together. I don't think they ever completely forgave either one of us.

Don't tell your mother I told you.

Pink Cadillac

Susan Whitmore

The photograph shows Uncle Donny draped across his '66 Cadillac Eldorado. Gumtrees and yellow grass in the background, a quintessentially Australian backdrop. His exotic cars were a frequent sight zipping up and down the east coast, towing an assortment of oversized caravans not infrequently decked out with antiques, a swinging chandelier or two, and on one memorable occasion, a live lamb.

The lamb was a familiar story told by Uncle Donny: as a doctor, patients often gave him gifts, quid pro quo. On another occasion, and I don't know how he'd helped this particular patient, his Cadillac went from rusty green to pink glimmering dream. It wasn't quite the cotton candy pink he'd hoped for, less Elvis Rose and more Mary Kay, but it was, most definitely, pink.

"Doesn't she look fab-u-lous," Uncle Donny caressed the bonnet, a long pink shimmer at the top of our grey suburban driveway. "And wait, there's more…" He put on a chauffeur's cap, covering his bleached tips. "Ready to take Mademoiselle to the school formal."

Up close, the pink was more mottle than shimmer and the driver's window refused to close. But I loved it, and the man who'd driven from Brisbane to Canberra just to drive me the ten minutes to the formal. The 14-hour trip had taken 48; his boyfriend Eric grumbled they'd only popped out for milk. That was Uncle Donny to a T: the ordinary always became an adventure, and never when you expected. I didn't even want to go to the formal, but there was no way I was telling him.

"Life's all about the entrance," said Uncle Donny sweating under the summer sun beside the Cadillac, the fattest, funniest, most divine human I ever met. "Be a memory. Be a pink Cadillac when everyone else is a grey Honda. Sprinkle a little sparkle." Fingers fluttering in the air as he spoke.

My hairstyle didn't make it past the end of our street, we stopped twice to top up the oil, and one 'Elvis 1' number plate flew off, but we definitely made an entrance. Pink glitter in a sea of black stretched limos. Eric, top half chauffeur, bottom half board-shorts, jumped out to open the door. My two friends and I swept out, movie stars for a moment, posing against the pink.

Canberra, 1995. Bland as its concrete heart, inexcusably dull: even graffiti failed to create a sense of devious excitement. So it didn't take much to convince my sister and me to drive back to Brisbane in the Cadillac. The lack of air-conditioning and dodgy brakes should have worried us, not to mention the petrol fumes that permeated the backseat whenever the motor started. But we were teenagers, and six weeks of school holidays stretched out before us, an unblemished blue sky.

The sun was already hot and high when we climbed into the back seat. Uncle Donny heaved into the front next to Eric. The engine spluttered to life. Our parents' concerned figures waved us off. I opened the jellybeans before we had even turned the corner.

Five hours, too many jellybeans and three petrol stops later we made it to Sydney. The Cadillac guzzled oil like an alcoholic and pissed it out in a steady stream. Occasionally, the traffic behind disappeared in a hiccup of black smoke. We waved at passing drivers who honked and hollered; it's not every day that you get stuck behind a pink Cadillac merging onto the M5.

At an intersection in Kings Cross, a white Mercedes pulled alongside. A fabulous blonde woman leaned across zebra skin seats.

"Hey, your Caddy for sale?"

"Depends. How much you offering?"

"Ten grand."

Traffic lights turned green. Cars began to honk. She pointed to an alley, gunned the motor and cut across the traffic. Uncle Donny waited for the green filter then rumbled off in pursuit.

"Could be interesting. If she offers fifteen we'll sell and all fly to Brisbane. What do you think, girls?" We nodded, stuffing Twisties into our mouths. Eric grunted.

In the alley, she circled the Cadillac and smiled in through the back window. We stopped stuffing our faces momentarily to smile back.

"She's a little rough, but I like it rough. Ten grand, final offer." Rolling r's, fluttering eyelids, licking lips.

"No way to negotiate with an old queer," Eric mumbled.

"I was thinking fifteen…"

She held up her hand. "When I say rough, I mean rough. There's a trail of oil all the way back home …"

"Let me confer with mis amigos." Uncle Donny stuck his head through the window. She waited, ten grand on her passenger seat, the ultimate negotiator.

"Push her to fifteen," Eric said. "I'm getting attached to the Caddy."

"You're just getting comfortable. Ten grand's ten grand."

"I don't get out of a car for less than fifteen."

"Me neither," I piped up.

"That's the spirit. Never settle for less than you're worth. Righto, I'll see what I can do... Oh..."

A car stopped in the alley. Two cops got out, tugging up belts, hats on heads, radios murmuring.

"Officers, good afternoon," Uncle Donny walked towards them.

We couldn't hear what was said, but a pink Cadillac and a woman with ten grand in an alley probably didn't look too innocent. Moments later she drove off. The cops followed.

"Appears the sale is a no-go." Uncle Donny got into the car and turned the key. Click. Tried again. Click. Eric refilled the oil.

He tried again.

Ka-boom.

"Too much oil?"

Uncle Donny shrugged, "Girls, it seems our story ends here, in an alley in Kings Cross."

"Classy way to end," Eric laughed.

The hired grey Honda chewed up the miles to Brisbane. No longer passengers in a spectacle of pink, we drove unnoticed in the crawling traffic, playing cat-and-mouse with the truck carrying the Cadillac.

"My love is bigger than a Honda," Eric and Uncle Donny sang from the Springsteen classic, whenever we overtook the Cadillac on the back of the truck. "No offence, Honda."

Magnets

Helen Chambers

"No-one saw us leave together, sneaking out like fugitives," he tells me.

"It was so different in the 80s," he says.

"AIDS shadowing my every move. We all knew people, of course. And I was so young, straight out of school, away at University. A fine crust of snow carpeted the city streets, worn thin into rutted ice. Stained by the day's traffic, it twinkled and glittered yellow and deceptive in dim pools of streetlight. I skidded on black ice; excitement expanding upwards from my stomach, tingling past my racing heart, prickling in my fingertips, resisting the pull-together, not quite touching, like magnets repelling but not repelled.

"In the pub, his cheeks burned healthy and wholesome in the glow from the open fire, and maybe something more. I don't remember which beer we drank, the nutty hops warm in the back of my mouth. I didn't even like beer. Crisps spilled from the red packet onto the polished table top and we reached for them at the same time, our hands not quite touching for a second too long and I thought my heart would stop beating. I held onto my breath and submerged in the warmth of his dark eyes and the comfort of his shy laugh. He held his hands to the fire, telling me how cold they were, and I lined mine up beside his, not quite touching, and we laughed as we wiggled our fingers like children.

"Wandering around the city after the pubs closed, I felt alive and spilled almost all my secrets, telling him everything I knew, all but the one thing that mattered, and he drank my words like he was thirsty for them. Knowing and not-quite knowing.

"Let's say we lost track of what time it was, for tomorrow and yesterday ceased to exist and even the chiming Town Hall clock meant nothing. Nothing mattered except walking in step, my coat sleeve brushing against his ski jacket sleeve, but not quite touching. That and not wanting to go back in where the others were. We kept on walking, our hot breaths steaming in front of us, mingling together into the thickening fog which hid our tracks, even from ourselves."

Family Matters

Carolyn Cordon

He was my once loved Uncle, but these days, with his hairy red bearded face, and brooding moods, together with distinctly yokel ways, well, I suspect we were all tiring of him. From his tatty coat, to his smoky stench, our love for him would shrink as we shrank from him.

Now though, here he was, wearing a fez, of all things, and softly humming to himself, a current tune. This was a hoot, my dowdy old uncle was turning hip! I rushed over to him, wanting to hug the silly old thing.

He held out his arm to stop me, 'Not now baby, I gots things to do.'

Then he picked up a tea cup and spoon, from those my mother had set out, for the gathered guests. He stepped forward, away from me, tapped the cup loudly, and cleared his throat. 'OK youse all, I'm here, youse is here, it's time to get some stuff sorted out. This is my house, right?' He thrust his chest forward, like he was ready to pick a fight.

The gathered masses either nodded, or looked confused, depending on how into the family politics they were. I'd always known Uncle Bert actually owned 'our' house. My mum looked after the house for my uncle, as he wandered around the place, coming back from time to time, to play some music, or get the ladder out to brood in the attic for a while, and to be called down in time for lunch or tea.

It has worked well for my mother and me, and for her brother, my uncle, too, as far as I could tell. So what was going on now, I wondered … Uncle Bert cleared his throat, and the quizzically murmuring guests quietened.

'OK,' he began, 'I's got some news here, you might not like it, you might not give two hoots, but here it is. I's got meself a wife!'

Now the noise level jacked up even higher: shrieks, a few guffaws, and much shaking of heads at what was going on. My uncle waved his hands, seemingly to quash the noise. 'I'm a man you know, and well, I thought my search was never gonna be successful, but I kept at it and kept at it, and I found her, or she found me, and geez, I got's me a bewdy!'

He put his fingers to his lips and whistled, loudly, like he used to do when he was doing his sheep herding. I looked at my uncle, then at my mum, shaking my head. He couldn't marry a kelpie, could he? But the woman who walked into the room, was no dog, she was a beauty! She strolled in, left hand held out in front, to display the enormous jewel on her ring finger, it looked familiar, then my mum saw it, and recognised it too.

'My opal! You've given away my opal, you creep!' she shouted, and leapt at the ring on the woman's hand. 'That's mine, you thieving bitch!'

I'd never ever heard my mum say a rude word, and I doubt any of the others had either, judging by the shocked faces all around. My uncle and several others held Mum back, but she was spitting and twisting like an angry cat. The 'bitch' smiled a slight smile, and nodded her head.

'He said his sis wouldn't be very happy about me having this ring,' she said. 'See Bert, just like I told you, she does want the opal.' She carefully removed the ring from the little finger of her hand, and approached my mother, now her sister-in-law. 'This is yours, if you want it. I think opals bring bad luck.'

And with that, she left, smile still on her rather lovely face, and reached out her hand to my Uncle Bert. 'Come on hubby, let's go where we're wanted! Lovely meeting you all, I'm Jeza, by the way, Jezabel, and this house is now mine, so look after it for me please.' With that, she held out her hand to "hubby", reached around with her other hand, and pinched his bum, then they headed toward the door.

'Enjoy the party!' they both called, and were gone.

Then the talk started, adult talk, and the Jezabel's height was much spoken of, and her deep voice too. I'd liked her voice, it seemed warm and friendly, but then, the clues suddenly merged, and I had it. We'd talked about the new laws, letting gay people marry each other, that had passed in Australia recently, in school, and I could suddenly see why my Uncle Henry had never found the woman of his dreams.

We'd often wondered about Uncle Henry and his ways, but finally some things were sliding into place. Of course he'd never found the lady to marry, he was never looking for a woman. It seemed my Uncle Henry was my gay Uncle Henry, and that was fine by me!

I was glad he'd found the person of his dreams though, and I hoped they'd both come back and visit sometime soon. Everyone crowded around Mum, demanding some answers, but she just shook her head, silently. I knew her better than anyone else though. We'd lived together, always, in our house, my uncle's house, Jeza's house? Mum had that look on her face, the one she got when she picked a 'Q' at scrabble when she already had a 'U' and a 'Z'. The one she got when she found a fifty dollar note in an Op Shop handbag's secret pocket.

Life was looking good, and any worries about babies arriving in Uncle Henry's immediate family could finally disappear. The home was ours, for sure, it seemed. And Auntie Jezabel could become my new favourite Aunt! I hoped she'd teach me how to do makeup, my mum was always too boring with these things, and it looked like Auntie Jezabel didn't mind going over the top, with many things!

Gaylord of the Dance

Colleen Moyne

In his younger years, my Uncle Steve was a dance instructor at
Fred Astaire Dance studios. Apparently, he was the most
attractive and popular teacher among the ladies who attended.
(I'll take his word for that.) The way he tells it, they would
hover around him like butterflies hoping to be the one chosen to
partner him – any excuse to run their hands over his taut,
athletic body.

There was one particular lady, though, who practically
stalked him. She would arrive early and leave late hoping for
any opportunity to be near him.

Despite his lack of interest, she seemed convinced that her
blatant flirting would win him over, and although instructors
were expected to stroke the egos of their students and
compliment them on their progress, Steve had to mind his words
around this lady for fear of leading her on.

At the time – and we are talking about fifty years ago –
sexual harassment of men by women was not even in the known
vocabulary and reporting her persistent behaviour was not an
option for him. Gay instructors were discouraged from
disclosing their personal information (which included their

sexual orientation) to patrons of the studio and she was far too smitten to catch on.

This blatant pursuit went on for several months, until one particular day when Steve and his partner Alex were having coffee in their local café. They happened to spot the woman from dance class entering and saw a fortuitous opportunity to solve Steve's problem.

Locking themselves in an intimate embrace there in the booth, they kissed passionately, only stopping when the woman – and several other patrons of the café – gasped audibly. The woman quickly turned and left, as expected, and from that day onward, gave Uncle Steve a cold reception every time she saw him. Her amorous attentions soon turned to another instructor at the studio who was also gay. No lesson learned there.

Steve didn't care. He was relieved to be left alone.

Consequently though, Steve and Alex were banned from the local café, but in his words, it was "totally worth it!"

Down Tunnels

Alisdair Hodgson

If you're to come out with me tonight, best tell you about last night first.

So, picture, it's a dark night int' tunnels. Got the side lights on, radio down at a whisper. Quieter out than the night before – maybe they know. Prozzies intuition. Still, it don't stop most of 'em. The fucking rapture wouldn't stop most of 'em, or their johns neither. Tosspots haunt these tunnels like lice, crawling up and down sniffing the air, wage packets burning through their jeans. Not that they get wage like that anymore, not since most the mines in the south were closed. I hear some of the prozzies take bank card now anyway.

But here, I can see faces. Can't usually see faces. Don't like seeing faces. Tunnels have more streetlamps since 'were last down, got cleaned an' all. Nice to see it kept tidy; nice place to sit and have bait box and brew. Only go when sun's out though.

Some oriental tyke chewing a mouthful of shit, neon skirt two inches from nasty, come skulking over to window as I roll the motor up t' kerb. Got window down a crack and she leers in, scoping the back and side seat for bonuses. No such luck.

"Hey thurrr." Scummy American. Fuck only knows how they import them.

"No ta, love," I says.

"Just a–" she says.

"No." I cut her off sharp-like. No point beating round bush and drawing notice. "Bad job, love. Move on, eh?"

She smirks, leers and swans off back t' hole she sprang out. Don't want anything to do with that. Got my eye on a pretty coloured one down the way. Her skin's like flecked granite. She's melons like man tits and an arse that wouldn't fill me hand. Perfect. My next causey princess. I drift down, past our Queen of Sheba, and bump up kerb in front of her. She looks hesitant, new, thirty maybe? They don't usually join the race at that late. Seems she don't know where to go. Figure I'll give her some directions. "Let's go, lass. Hop in."

She does and we negotiate, money up front. Wouldn't expect nothing less.

At house, back at mine I mean, she sits quiet-like. We 'ave a brew – she heaps on enough sugar to stand spoon in – and listen t' radio until me and the brew have bored her to sleep sideways on sofa. Utterly out for the count. Can't wait to hang this one next t' others.

I get kit out, laying my buckets; several pair of scissors, sharp and blunt, to keep things artistic; files and razor blades, all different sizes; and sponges, wipes and cloths to take care of the mess. I cut her clothes off and get to work on her. First the nails, one by one, always tricky to get a grip on from the years of daily coats they smear on. Then I work, happy but calm like, with the feet, privates, ears and hair, hacking away like a top bollocks chef. Last I do the face, which I've been waiting for, savouring temptation. I whistle for the lips, nice and tuneful through the nose, and devour each moment of her pretty green eyes, breathing it deep and storing it up for later.

And then, wouldn't you know, we're done. I dress the deconstructed girl int' dress I picked out in town, take a quick snap of her with polaroid, and admire my latest treasure. One for the books – and the wall. Yes, lad, that wall.

I crack the smelling salts, give her a whiff, and she's up and about looking like someone swanned in on Christmas and pissed on her sprogs. I take the little mirror off wall, round and face-size, and advance on her.

"Take a look, love. What do you think?"

Tell you how she looks, she looks a right presentable young lady, all neat and manicured. But, even at thirty, she's still a lamb and easy startled. Bolts straight out the door, she does, vanishing back into night, that pretty little dress blowing in the wind, leaving just an echo of a foreign accent, "Creep!" Maybe Nigerian or Welsh. She don't look like she belong on the streets no more.

Back t'tunnels tonight though. You'll see.

Don't know who'd save the lasses if it weren't for us.

Raspberry Raindrops

Henry Bladon

'The world isn't full of raspberry raindrops, kid.' The first time I recall my Uncle Trevor saying that was to my mum that time when he arrived soaking wet at our house. Mum gasped when she saw him and then dashed to grab a towel. At the time, I remember trying to work out why raindrops would be flavoured. Uncle Trevor took off his leather gloves and winked at me before shaking my hand. He didn't care about the rain. Nor did I, for that matter, I couldn't wait to get out to the beach and play football with him (although football, by his own admission, 'wasn't his thing'). Mum said, 'Your uncle has ridden on that clapped-out old motorbike for five hours in the rain just to come and see you, let him have a cup of tea first.' Uncle Trevor told her to stop fussing and after he lit a cigarette, we walked to the beach to run about after the ball for what seemed like hours. We only stopped when the heel of one of his cowboy boots flew off as he took a free-kick. I looked at him wondering whether it would be okay to laugh. He retrieved his heel and looked at it in his hand. Then he looked at me and said, 'Never mind, kid, let's get an ice cream and then see what you mother has for supper.' Then we set off with our ice creams as Uncle Trevor hobbled back home with his stricken boot.

I heard his favourite expression plenty of times growing up and gradually realised it had a more abstract significance than I had initially believed. I always appreciated the fact that he didn't say *seize the day*, or *don't let them grind you down*, and simply lug about a tired old platitude. Mum always said he was lucky because he was oblivious. 'He's an ostrich,' she would say, but I knew better. I could see that it was part of an irrepressible spirit. I always thought there should have been a second part to his expression, which would have said something about his glass being half-full, but that wasn't necessary, and he knew it.

Now it's just me and Uncle Trevor waiting together, and I can almost hear his expression echo in the dimly lit chapel. I wanted to come here and tell him thanks for all the fun times and the laughter, and for putting himself out when my dad wasn't about. I thank him for all the happy memories that you can't go back and invent if they were never there in the first place. My thoughts turn to when I went to visit Uncle Trevor for the last time. Typically, all he was concerned about was how I was doing. He refused to talk about his illness, as if it were not there.

Tomorrow I'll be part of the crowd. Colourful friends and colleagues will meet up, everyone will say how full of life he was. Some people will talk about his ability to make them laugh; others will talk about his intellect and how he was such an influence on so many fellow scientists. Lifting out the big topics is what you do at times like this. For a moment, I wonder whether perhaps I should join in the clamour for the spotlight to shower post-life accolades on a celebrated individual, but I know Uncle Trevor never needed this acclamation. We will listen to his favourite music, which has been carefully selected, Peter will talk about the life they shared and how Trevor was his inspiration. People will cry as they always do at funerals. That's all for tomorrow, though. For now, as I leave the calm of the chapel and walk into the drab daylight, I look down at the faded photo of us with an ice cream on the beach and I smile. It starts to spot with rain, and for a brief moment I swear I have the taste of raspberry in my mouth.

My Gay Uncle Hilton

Chuka Susan Chesney

Your Favorite Uncle

Back in the '60s, whenever I threw my head back and laughed, you'd giggle at the shimmer of fillings in my teeth. Then I'd cough. My clothing and breath smelled like Lucky Strikes, but you didn't notice. You were too busy thinking about the rolls of Reed's candies I kept in my trouser pockets. I brought sweets to our family gatherings to disguise my breath, but your little girl self thought the candy was just for you. I kept my suckers hidden so we wouldn't have to share them with the adults.

As soon as I walked in, you ran to me and reached into my pockets. I had lots of flavors on hand – cinnamon, butterscotch and root beer. Each lozenge was individually wrapped in cellophane that opened with a delicious crinkly sound before we popped them in our mouths.

Kids' Table

When the meal was ready, we sat at the kids' table in the kitchen. The boring adults' table was crowded with chairs and serving dishes in the dining room. I was the baby of your mom's family, and enjoyed sitting with you where no one muttered, "tsk tsk." My brothers and sisters and their spouses didn't like me much. They suspected I was gay, and knew I smoked. I'd never married, lived with Mother for several years, and had a lot of odd jobs. Rumors swirled I was mentally ill. Plus, when I was a boy, I accidentally killed the family cow when I took her out to graze in some perilla mint weeds.

Christmas Presents

One Christmas, after lunch, your Nana Lillian grinned and handed you a package with wrinkled gift wrap. Two sheets of floral paper had been spliced together with tape. A used strand of curling ribbon was tied dejectedly around the box. You already knew to be wary of Nana. She used to yank your tangles with a comb while she French braided your hair. She drooled down her chin before she kissed you. Your father once told me she insisted on sleeping with you in your twin bed, but you said, "No! You stink!" You were eight years old when you opened the Christmas present from Nana. It was a huge baby doll with staring eyes and pursed, pink lips, the way a mortician prepares a dead face. Everyone gasped, "Oh! a doll!"

It was a gift for a much younger girl than you. You loved Barbies with pointy breasts, curvy legs, and fashion clothes. Then I gave you an enormous box wrapped in Rudolph the Red-nosed Reindeer paper. You tore it open and found a *Creepy Crawlers Thingmaker*. Batteries were included in a small package on the top. This time **you** gasped with joy! So did your brother and sister.

Creepy Crawlers

We hurried out to the front porch, pulling loot out of the box. There were metal molds of centipedes, scorpions, and other multi-legged insects. We spread them out on cement and lined up tubes of Plastigoop in neon colors – raspberry pink, glowworm green, neon orange, and popsicle blue. We poured Plastigoop into molds, setting them inside the electric hot plate *Creepy Crawlers* oven. I made sure you didn't burn your fingers. Pretty soon we had an assortment of rubbery toy bugs we'd made ourselves. We dropped them down each others' backs, and you piled them on my balding head. Then we discovered we could squirt gobs of different colors together into molds and make rainbow creatures. You looked at me and your eyes shone. You told me the toy I gave you was your favorite Christmas present.

Portrait

After a while I moved away to Colorado Springs to live with my artist lover Steve who painted a portrait of you from your 6th grade school picture. A package arrived at your door one day. Your mother told me you opened it, but I guess you were repelled by the realistic oil painting of your pre-adolescent self.

Your mother told you to hang the portrait in your room. Instead you wrapped it in a sheet and hid it under the bed.

Monosyllables

You only saw me a couple of times after that. I came to visit when you were in your early 20s. You hardly paid any attention to me. You barely spoke to anyone at that point. You were enrolled in a highly competitive design school, and had a serious boyfriend. I smiled and tried to talk to you, but you answered in monosyllables. I guess you felt you'd outgrown me like the huge doll Nana gave you. It had ended up in a pile of cast-offs in the basement.

Heart Attacks

A few years later, I was living with your Aunt Flora in Oklahoma, penniless. I had a stroke and passed away the same weekend your father died unexpectedly of a massive coronary. You never processed my death because you were reeling from the loss of your father. Aunt Flora was mad at me for dying in my early 60s. She said I would have lived a lot longer if I hadn't smoked, and that Christians shouldn't have vices. But she figured I went to heaven because I had the gift of speaking in tongues.

I was the second sibling in the family to die. The first was my brother Ross who died a noble death as a POW in World War II.

One Less Date

I wish we could go back to the time when I visited. Maybe you could have had one less date with your boyfriend and skipped that third set of swatches you painted in the middle of the night. I wanted to walk with you in the canyon underneath live oaks. Carrying flashlights, avoiding pairs of skunks grubbing beside storm drains. If we'd walked into a spider web, we would have brushed it aside. I could pass you a cinnamon candy. I still have one in my pocket.

My Gay Uncle the Sailor

DeLeon W. Peacock

My Uncle Leonard knew I was gay long before I did but he didn't mention it or even bring gay up in conversations other than when he wanted to talk about this guy he knew. Though it was never talked about, everybody in the family knew he was gay. There was just a way about him and the fact that he got along better with women than men. It appeared as though he never had a girlfriend and he loved to shop with a group of his women friends.

We lived in a very religious family where you were expected to go to church every time the doors were open and we never started a meal without saying a blessing. Fire and brimstone were the topic of the sermons three out of four Sundays each month. Our entire extended family attended the same church and were among the Sunday School teachers and deacons of the church. Sex outside marriage and especially homosexuality were among the top sins that would send your ass straight to hell. When my mother's youngest sister got pregnant by her boyfriend she was made to leave home and her name was never mentioned again. That left an indelible impression on me. My Uncle Leonard searched for her until he found her and became a part of her life by making sure she had everything she needed.

He told me the reason he joined the US Navy was because of the song by The Village People that spoke about the good times a man could have "In The Navy." I was about fourteen years old when Uncle Leonard came home from the Navy. He didn't have anywhere to live so his sister, my mother, allowed him to live with us. I could tell right off that he had changed in his attitude about life and toward everybody around him. He begin to act like he didn't really care if people knew he was gay or not. My mother didn't like this new attitude that my uncle displayed.

Uncle Leonard was a handsome man with a tall slim body and the face of an angel and he knew it. This became even more apparent to me after he came back from the Navy.

My mother was very protective of me because I think she may have known I was leaning toward the same lifestyle as my uncle. Mother had an idea that Leonard was gay but he was also her brother and she loved him.

I know my uncle was privy to my sexual difference because he had caught me eyeing the boys with lust in my eyes.

As we sat on the front porch together my uncle started telling me the story of his coming out. I had been expecting this ever since he'd gotten back because of the way his vocabulary had changed. I though he was talking a lot more gay-like than when he had left.

"Can you keep a secret? Can I tell you something and you not go blabbing it around?"

"I guess."

"No, you have to promise me. Do you promise?"

"OK, I promise. I guess."

"You remember me telling you why I went into the Navy?"

"Something about a song I think. I think it was a Navy song."

"It wasn't just any Navy song; it was the song by The Village People. You know who the Village People are, don't you?"

"I think so. Was it about young men having fun in the Navy? Aren't they the ones who sing about the YMCA?"

"Yea, you got it. Well, do you understand what kind of fun they were talking about?"

"I think I sorta do."

"So what do you think you sorta know?"

"It talks about having a good time while you're in the Navy."

Of course I knew what the song was about because it was one of my favorite songs that I had to sneak around to listen to but I wasn't going to be the first one to say the word "Gay."

"Sweet boy, I've never told anyone this before. I'm gay and the song is talking about having a gay good time "In the Navy." I went into the Navy because I'm gay and have always known it."

He had said the "Gay" word and I didn't know what to do or say in response. We both just sat there without a word for what seemed an eternity. I couldn't even look at him because the Lion had been let out of the cage and it was hungry.

I saw tears start rolling down his cheeks. When he told me he was gay he had said it in a whisper as though he knew when he told me it would change everything. I was the first person he had confided in and I had to keep it a secret from everyone.

What Uncle Leonard didn't know was that I had heard my mother arguing with my dad the night before. As I stood by their bedroom door my mother was crying and my dad was saying that Uncle Leonard had to leave because he was a bad influence on me. I told Uncle Leonard this and his tears flowed as though a river had opened up.

"It's ok, I've saved up enough money to get my own place. What are you going to do when they find out about you?"

I was silent.

"Sweet boy, have you not come to terms with the fact that you're gay?"

I got up from the porch chair and ran into the house. Mom and Dad were gone. I was so weak I couldn't make it up the stairs. Uncle Leonard put his arms around me.

When I turned sixteen my parents threw me out of the house and I moved in with Uncle Leonard and his partner.

Beer, bongs and bovver boots

Michèle Saint-Yves

It was 1984, in the space between night and dawn in the middle of the dry season. Mum and I had landed in Darwin from the UK to join my Dad and older brother.

Even at that hour, I walked out into an air that suffocated me as if a wet plastic bag had been pulled over my head. The tarmac seemed to melt my plimsolls, as we walked into a terminal of cheap Besser block and corrugated iron that stank of sweat and stale fuel recycled by the clicking overhead fans. My mother didn't give the best of hellos to the rest of her men folk.

And if Darwin was anything, it was a town for men folk. A population of 60,000 and eight males for every female. It was a town of transients serving three industries: mining, defence and trade. In fact, everything about Darwin came as a trinity: meat pies, sauce and Farmers Union Iced coffee; Darwin Hotel, Casino and Travelodge; Darwin, Casuarina and Dripstone High Schools; and, beer, bongs and gunja.

But my teenager trinity were the places that lay at the centre of Darwin's nightlife – Dicks, Boobies and Fannies. The holiest of these was Fannies. This was the place where I found my people cloistered and where we made and practiced our own rituals. A place where practices were not seen as sacrilegious but of brother/sister-hood love.

Darwin was too small to maintain separate subcultures and it was Fannies that served as the altar for those with an alternative bent. On the bottom floor was the dance floor, taking up most of the space, with a bar and dark nooks to drink. To go up to the next floor, you ascended a wide spiral staircase that was broken up midway by the DJ booth with two turntables. The top floor had long tables, brighter lighting and a glass balcony overlooking the dance floor. Each distinct space of the club was claimed by a subculture and we all crossed over at the bar and at the DJ booth. There were the Goths, the New Romantics, the Ska mob, the Punks, the Mods, The Escorts and The Gays. Every Wednesday and Thursday night we could bring our own records for the DJ to play and so we also cross-overed in our music and dance styles. And it is where I began my own cross-over.

Within six months of 'adjusting' to Darwin (using Darwinism as a metaphor is just too obvious!), I had become best mates with a Mod. His best mate was a Punk and they both had their hair done by another good mate – an openly flamboyant gay man – and the first 'known' gay I'd met. We would meet at his salon every month for bleaching, dyeing and shaving. And, because of this unusual band of brothers, I would go to Mod bar parties, Punk band parties and gay male house parties. But the Punk and I were not mates, as we were never alone outside of these times.

Gradually there formed a core at the centre of this Venn diagram of these seemingly disparate subcultures. It flexed in size from a dozen to two dozen, with an equal representation of

Mods, Punks, New Romantics, Ska and gay boys. Sometimes clusters from this core would go off to dinners, camping weekends or backyard barbies with mates from the invitee's tribe.

I was dating a 'classic Aussie beauty', but unbeknownst to her or my friends, I regularly had one-night stands with men who were in town for business or holiday. They were usually over twenty-five and straight and I came to know the rooms of the YMCA and Travelodge rather well. Then it happened – I became emotionally attached to a boy in the Fannies scene.

Everyone knew him: he was that chiselled jaw surfie-hunk type with a confidence that escaped me, who knew anyone there was to know, who dealt gunja and uppers-&-downers and lived in a townhouse with the air steward pretty boys. It jump-started one day at the mall after school when he surprised me by calling out my name from JUST JEANS. He invited me for coffee and introduced me to a cappuccino. Let's just say I have not been able to drink a cappuccino in quite the same way again.

And that cappuccino experience led me to spend less and less time in the Mods subculture and to begin to hang out more with The Gays. It was noticed.

It was the Punk's birthday and he invited eight of us Mods and Punks to a meal at a restaurant. We had hung out loads of times but there was a tension this night. I noticed a huddling around the table that left my best mate and I spaced away from the rest. Then out it came: 'Why did you invite HIM the Homo?' 'He's a fuckin' dirty queer!' 'Better fuckin' not touch me!' 'Filthy poofter!' 'Fucking freak', 'Fairy'. That's how it sounded anyway. As I descended into mortification, I turned to my best mate but he said nothing, not a thing. Then out of nowhere came this: 'If you don't apologise to him right now and shut the fuck up with that shit you can leave. And don't expect to be invited to anything by me again.' Anyway, that's what I believe I heard. The Punk became my King.

The next time I saw my King was at his house for the next Punk band party. I didn't have the right outfit it seems for, as people were about to arrive, he looked me up and down, shook his head and silently went into his room. He returned with his prized cherry Doc Martens and said 'Ya better fuckin' catch these' as he went off. My best mate simply said: 'Fuck, he never lets anyone wear his bovver boots.'

Apocalypse

E. M. Stormo

On New Year's Eve, I stayed up all night to make sure the world didn't end. My parents went to a Mayan-themed costume party and left me home with Uncle Ron. Dad called him "gay Uncle Ronnie," even though Dad was dressed in feathers and a loincloth. Mom called him plain "Uncle Ronnie," but we were already on a first-name basis. "Just call me Ron," he said last New Year's. " 'Uncle Ron' makes me sound like a pedophile."

Dick Clark was on TV, although I thought he died. He was about to die again. Dick the divine sacrifice. The Times Square ball hung over the city like an atom bomb. Would it get a chance to explode before the aliens invaded, or the no-name asteroid hit the Earth and scattered us like ants off an apple? Fire or ice—whichever horse it rode upon, the apocalypse would trample over everyone equally. There was nothing left to do but sit and watch TV, and wait for it.

Red-toothed Ron finished a bottle of wine before ten. 2012 was still two hours off. I promised myself I'd remain conscious until morning came. I didn't want to sleep through it, even if it was just void and there was nothing to experience. Only adults wish to die in their sleep. Ron and I would be seated upright for the moment of truth, him comfy in the recliner, me nervously folded up on the couch.

The Twilight Zone marathon proved too much for me. A bookworm lost his glasses in a nuclear holocaust. A woman passed out from global warming, only to find she was dreaming and the world was really undergoing global cooling.

Ron called me a "hypersensitive child," before switching back to Dick Clark. As the night wore on, Dick appeared to undergo zombification. He was about to herald the year's end for the last time. Every micro-gesture winked the inevitable. Our deaths were upon us.

Around eleven, Ron shut off the TV. "This is lame. Let's play a game." He laughed at his unintentional rhyme, then knelt at the bookshelf to rifle through the boardgames.

"*Life*, pass; *Sorry*, bleh; *Monopoly*, oy! How about cards?"

"Can I see one of your books?"

Ron patted himself down. "I don't have any."

"Why not?"

"They're all online."

"Show me on your phone."

"No."

"What's it called?"

"It's not under my real name, and I'll never tell you!"

"Why not?"

"Because your mom wouldn't approve. I don't write stories for children."

I lowered my voice. "I'm not a child."

"You're scared of *The Twilight Zone*. You're scared of Dick Clark!"

"The world is ending tonight."

Ron made a deal with me. If I could procure another bottle of wine, he'd reveal the plot of one of his books. Dad kept an old jug of Manischewitz in the China cabinet for Passover, but he had forgotten about it for years. I showed Ron the jug; it was more wine than any man could drink in one night.

"To the End of the World," he said while toasting my hot chocolate.

"Don't say that." I checked the clock. We were in the dreadful elevens.

"Alright. Your mom's gonna kill me. She doesn't even know my pen-name. My best-seller is about a man who falls in love with a bear."

"A bear?"

"Yes, they meet, fall in love, and go back to his cave. The end. You know what happens next. Basically a gender-swapped Marian Engel."

"What do they do in the cave?"

"They have sex, dummy. Don't all ten year-olds look at porn?"

I shook my head.

"Bless you, innocent child." Ron made a clumsy sign of the cross like a left-handed vampire.

"Isn't that *bestiality?*"

"Technically 'erotica'. Technically 'gay male erotica written by gay men', not to be confused with 'gay male erotica written by straight women'."

I didn't know what he meant, but his Manischewitz mustache made me giggle.

"Your mom is going to murder me."

"How many books do you have?"

"Oh, eighty or so. Maybe a hundred. I lost count. They're all bad, like phenomenally bad. I can't even remember them all. Not one of them could be called literature, even in the broadest sense."

"What's your favorite book?"

"My favorite of mine? I can't tell you the title, but it's about a man who gets abducted by aliens. They take him back to the mothership. They fall in love. The end. I had a lot of fun writing the sex scenes in that one. I researched a lot of anime. You really never watch that stuff?"

I shook my head in disgust.

"It ain't Shakespeare. Willy's far more flowery than I and more perverse too. I could write a real book, you know. Well, shit." Ron held up the jug as level as he could. It was half-empty.

"Don't say that."

"What? *Shit?*"

"Yes."

"You blessèd child." Uncle showed me a rare sign of affection by patting me on the head. "I apologize for my crude words."

"I'd read your book."

"Sadly, the homo-avuncular genre is oversaturated at the moment. Oh, hey! Look at that! It's already 12:02. We missed it. Happy New Year then."

"Happy New Year." I mouthed the words, but I didn't believe.

"Guess the Mayans were *meshugge*."

"Yeah, guess so." I studied the clock to see if time had stood still, but it was just me frozen on the couch.

"You sound disappointed." Ron joked around, but the old year wouldn't let me go. 2011 had yet to have its way with me. The clock hands held me in place. The couch arms wrapped around my torso. Residual white noise from the TV hypnotized me into believing I was awake despite being unconscious. Dick Clark was no help. He had died the previous spring.

I was like one of Ron's characters in his books. I had fallen in love with apocalypse. I had gone back to apocalypse's place. You know what happens next.

The Secret

Melisa Quigley

When Uncle Bob turned twenty his parents disowned him because he told them he was gay. He moved out of home and for a decade no one heard from him except me. He wouldn't tell me where he was living. He just needed someone to talk to who would listen. He told me he was sexually assaulted by a neighbour just after his twelfth birthday. His parents went out and left their neighbour, Max, to mind him and his younger sister. His sister fell asleep and Max cornered my uncle in the bedroom when he was changing to get ready for bed.

He was too frightened to tell his parents because he said they'd think he was lying. It was our secret which he told me never to tell anyone. I didn't tell him that I couldn't keep secrets. I had to tell someone – anyone who would listen. I told Mum.

'Uncle Bob has a vivid imagination,' she said. 'Don't believe anything he tells you.'

He rang two weeks later, and I told him I was having trouble with my girlfriend. She nagged me for a friendship ring, but I didn't want to buy one for her.

'Girls are opinionated and bitchy,' he said. 'Having you should be enough.'

For years we would talk on the phone. The word 'gay' was forbidden in our house, but Mum always wanted to know what was happening.

'If you turn out to be like your uncle, you're not welcome back,' said Dad. 'Your uncle's a dirty bugger.'

Uncle Bob didn't care what other people said about him. He was in a relationship with another man.

'Don't hide behind who you are. I used to date girls to make my parents happy. You can't live your life behind a façade forever. People will find out eventually. Be true to you.'

Uncle Raymond

Chris Hall

One day at a family gathering I found myself blurting out, "Uncle Raymond, why are you gay?"

He laughed and quickly retorted, "Why are you not?"

A question I realised I could not rightly answer.

Then my father piped in, "Because your Uncle Raymond is perverted and you're not."

Uncle Raymond nodded, "Of course my brother, your father, has known me a lot longer than anyone else, so he should know." Then he pulled up a seat next to mine and proceeded to provide me with a concise explanation.

"In 1952, the American Psychiatric Association listed homosexuality as a mental disorder in the Diagnostic and Statistical Manual. In those days it was generally believed that anyone who engaged in overt acts of perversion lacked the emotional stability of a normal person.

"A study of homosexuality in 1962 was used to justify its inclusion with the explanation it is a hidden pathological fear of the opposite sex caused by a traumatic parent–child relationship." He looked up at my father, "Isn't that right, Ted?" Father said nothing. He continued. "Your dad wouldn't agree with the trauma part, because it turns out our father was a pretty chill dude. Of course, the psychiatrists worked out how to fix this problem with the use of electroshock therapy, designed to decrease same-sex attraction, but when they figured out that didn't work, and protesting gays were getting arrested left right and centre, they figured the game was up and removed homosexuality from the Diagnostic and Statistical Manual in December 1973.

"In those days gays were humiliated and despised, and unlike other underprivileged groups, such as women, blacks, and Jews, who struggled for respect and equal rights, homosexuals had nothing that physically identified them as unique."

I was so intrigued to find out how it would have been possible for him to "come out" in the anally retentive sixties; I asked my flamboyant gay uncle exactly how he managed it. I was surprised to discover how enthused and forthcoming he was to educate me about such matters. "I imagine you couldn't tell your parents in those days."

He nodded. The following is what he told me. "It was difficult for most to come out. Our parents grew up in oppressive times; they didn't understand our need to assert our individuality."

"So how did you go about it?"

"Not knowing how our dad would react," he answered, "I one day summed up the courage to announce my orientation, and it went something like this ..."

"Dad, I have something serious to tell you."

"That's a bit ominous," he replied, *"do you think I should sit down for this?"*

"Absolutely."

He picked the most comfortable armchair he could find, one he couldn't fall out of, and said, "Ok, go!"

"I'm gay."

He frowned, shook his head and whispered, "Thank the Lord for that."

"What?" I responded, confused.

He smiled. "I thought you were going to tell me something serious like, you'd got a girl pregnant." He drew in a deep breath. "At least that's one less thing I have to worry about now."

"Well yes," I admitted, "I guess that's unlikely to happen."

"Good," he sighed, "is that it then?"

"Eh, yes," came my stunned reply, "I suppose so."

He stood up and walked toward the door. As if it were an afterthought he turned and said, "Anyway, the customary family rule still applies."

"What's that?" I asked.

"No sex before marriage."

"But this is the sixties," I replied, "Gays can't marry."

He shrugged, "That's hardly my fault; I don't make the rules."

Grappling for a response, I blurted out. "But it is the age of free love."

He regarded me quizzically. "I once tried telling your mother that; nine months later she had you, and you've cost me a fortune. Nothing comes for free."

Once he had finished his tale Uncle Raymond grinned sardonically. I wasn't sure how to take him, so I asked, "What about your mother, how did you tell her?"

"I didn't," he replied, "Dad beat me to it."

"How?"

"He said to her, I think it might be time for Raymond to come out of the closet."

"I agree," she responded, "but he's a bit late. All those clothes that are strewn around his room have beaten him to it."

My Rainbow Man

RubinA

It's a gloomy day. Not because it's been raining since morning, nor because I am walking through the hospital corridors to meet my Uncle Sam who has been off and on artificial life support for the past three days. This man I am going to meet has the power to change the way I feel, despite the fact that he is lying powerless on the hospital bed counting his last moments. He was a great storyteller. Did I just mention him... in past tense? Reality is cruel. It hits you even before it has actually happened. 'Think positive,' I tell myself. And without realizing I enter his room. I told you, this man has the power to change the way I think. I enter with a smile. I quietly approach his bed and sit down on a chair. His bed is near a window. Clouds have made way for the sun but it's drizzling still. I can't stop myself from touching my uncle's hand. Without any intention of disturbing him I just lay my hand on his. In a flash of a second I recall all the stories that he told me, like, 'Fish lives in water because she's shy,' 'Trees eavesdrop,' 'Earth and sky are lovers.' After this one I had told him that it's land and not earth, Earth is our planet and we walk on land, but he had persisted that it's earth. And there was another one, about Rainbow.

*

I recall a seven-year-old me sitting with my uncle on the porch of my grandfather's house. We all had come to celebrate Easter with him. A beautiful day it was. Happy faces, that distinct smell of cinnamon coming from the oven, fresh flowers sitting on the table, music in the background and my cousin Henry showing off his moves to those songs. It didn't matter to him that those were holy prayers. He just danced. I learnt to take notice of all these beautiful things around me because of my uncle. He would talk to me about feathers and butterflies, about clouds and the skies, leaves and the flowers, about rainbows and the showers. He had always been a fresh change for me from my father who talked only of facts. I enjoyed my uncle's company more which my father did not really like much. Because, Uncle Sam was an artist and he was gay. Throughout my childhood I believed that my father disliked him because he was an artist. But, it wasn't so.

That day, I was sitting with my uncle and we were looking at the sky. I was not doing it by choice. Uncle Sam had made me sit and look at the sky. I had had a fight with my cousin Henry over... nothing significant. We both were high on holidays, I believe. That day we couldn't play outdoors because it was raining off and on. Just as Uncle Sam and I sat on the porch a big rainbow appeared. 'Hey! Look!' I pointed at the rainbow excitedly. 'Aha, Rainbow!' he said. I saw a spark in his eyes as bright as mine. I took a second to judge him for being equally excited. Grown-up men don't react like that. My father never did. He asked me, 'Do you know why it appears?' I told him that rainbow formation is taught in Grade five and I was still in

Grade two. I remembered Henry showing off his knowledge about the phenomenon when I had dared to touch a rainbow poster in his room. He showered his rain crystals on me and passed light through them. And I uttered the same words in no specific order. 'Bullshit!' he reacted louder than I expected. 'I know, I don't know the exact words to describe that process,' I told him, a little disappointed in myself for not remembering it as Henry had told. But then, I had not listened carefully to him either when he was enlightening me. 'I haven't asked you when it appears. I asked you why it appears,' said Uncle. I did not even understand that these two questions were different from each other in any way. I just looked at him, choosing not to say anything meaningless and make a fool of myself. 'What would you do when someone offers you a drink you really need, without using any words at all?' He set me thinking. 'I think I would accept readily with a big smile.' Uncle Sam was scribbling with a colored pen on paper. He showed it to me. A smile was drawn on it. 'Like this?' he asked. I looked at it. 'Yeah! Maybe,' I shrugged. He drew six more smiles, some under and some above that one and inverted the paper and showed again. 'What do you think this is?' I looked at the paper and looked at the rainbow again. The basic structure matched and as a seven-year-old I tried to make sense of this mixed conversation about science and art by blurting, 'A Rainbow?'

'You got it!' said he, making me feel like a winner. 'Rainbow is earth smiling at the sky when it is showered love without conditions, and the sun witnessing that gesture.'

I was so impressed, I think for life. Whatever stories he told me have taught me some wise and beautiful things.

There can be different truths to one fact. You can choose your truth to create your own reality.

Think beyond the obvious.

Shifting focus in hard times can lift you up again.

As I am recalling this I feel his hand squeeze mine. A little surprised, I look at him with a smile. He points at the window. A rainbow has splashed across the sky. We both look at each other and smile, feeling the earth smiling too.

Uncle Lee

Tom Fegan

Uncle Lee lost both legs serving as a U.S. Army Ranger in the Viet Nam War. And he kept his sexuality secret from the Army. "Not their business," he claimed. Otherwise, Uncle Lee never hid the fact he was gay. Additionally, his sister (my mother) and her boyfriend (my father) all had protested the War and experienced Woodstock. Although children of the Sixties, they were drug and alcohol-free when I came along, but they continued their politically liberal but morally conservative actions. Mom and Dad got married when I was in first grade.

Dad and Uncle Lee dropped out of college and signed up. Dad was an Army Medic. Mom explained to me it was the balance of Yin and Yang between them: Dad saved lives by healing and Uncle Lee saved lives by fighting. A landmine claimed his legs. He rejected prosthetic legs, preferring a wheelchair. "I earned these wheels!" he joked. Mom finished her degree in philosophy and taught Tai Chi at home. Dad worked as a mechanic.

The three of them purchased a duplex to maintain family unity yet have their own space. Dexter Chang, a much younger

Asian male, was Lee's partner. Mom told me it was special that I had two uncles.

Unlike most boys, Mom instructed me not only in Tai Chi but paralleled it with Eastern Philosophy. She favored the Tao Te Ching. Lao Tzu became my favorite philosopher over Confucius. I studied the Bible as well and Uncle Lee indulged me with his stories which always included life lessons. In warm weather we would sit on the front porch and from his wheelchair he expounded his tales; otherwise we would sit inside with the television off for his oratory.

One summer evening he told a tale that remained fermenting within me. It centered on a caterpillar he captured and placed in a jar for his third grade class "Show and Tell" day. "Mrs. Porter told me," he began, "She said, 'Lee, it's best to release it back into nature and become a butterfly and serve its purpose to bring beauty into this world. Its role is to do that, as each and every living thing has its own role. We do too. Nature serves our needs and we in turn should serve and protect it.'"

"It really registered with me what she said," he continued, "And so at recess I opened the jar and set it free." He hesitated a moment.

"Then what happened?" I asked.

"Well," he drew a deep breath then spoke, "At the time we had a classroom bully by the name of Freddie Miller and he stomped on that poor creature and craned his head back, chuckling loud as he could."

"And?" I leaned forward with interest.

"I hit him hard as I could in his belly and knocked him backwards with an upper cut. He hit the pavement and was laid out. Mrs. Porter ran over and checked him out. He recovered."

"Wow, Uncle Lee. You knocked him out."

"I did. He went to the school nurse and I went to the principal. Then the principal saw him alone and then both of us together." I continued to listen. "We parted friends." I was puzzled and he explained. "You see nephew, I learned something that day."

I listened closely as he explained. "That principal reiterated what Mrs. Porter had said: that life is precious and not to be wasted or terminated needlessly. He pointed at me and told me that when something happens to me that is a personal affront, take proper action and go to an authority figure. Self defense is okay only when necessary."

Uncle Lee paused. "Freddie Miller and his family moved at the end of the year but we were buddies at school until he left." My inquisitive expression made him smile. "You see," he replied, "Freddie's parents were always fighting and threatening to divorce. His dad would leave for a few days and return. They were a military family so they moved a lot."

"He really didn't have any friends, did he," I said.

Uncle Lee nodded. "Right. Some of what I learned that day was we never know what the other person is going through. So be as nice as you can to all." Of all his stories, that was the one that stuck in my memory, as I grew, and attended college and pursued a career in Human Resources.

I wouldn't trade my childhood with my parents, the duplex and Uncle Lee and Dexter. Outside looking in, I know others shook their head in bewilderment as to how we lived. "Hippies," I overheard us called. Love was the center of our world and I learned to share it.

He Would Say

Alex Reece Abbott

Over a glass of watery orange cordial, my uncle would laugh and ask if you'd seen him wave that day.

That day yonks ago, summer sun searing, no *Hurricane* fencing, no health and safety on the rugged site. And you, a toddler standing stock still at the edge of the cavity, staring into the guts of the earth.

Watching him circling in his massive *Caterpillar*, the colour of a burnished poppy, bumping over the scraped ochre clay, overwhelmed by the gigantic scale of the open cast mine. The handsome captain at the helm, manoeuvring the iron beast on the greasy track, extracting black gold for the new power station down the river.

You'd squinted hard at him in his glass cage…had he seen you? You'd waved to him till your arm ached, then stopped. If you distracted him, he could slide and tumble into the gaping crater.

It's a man's world of men's men. Plenty of singlets and shorts, sweat and swagger, boots and boozing and swearing around the camp. The air perfumed with diesel and *Golden Virginia*, the growl of heavy machinery and the ring of dynamite in your ears. He's popular, a good bloke, reliable and not afraid of a hard day's yakka. They call him Paddy – a nickname is a good thing…right?

He fits in.

He stands out.

He is tall and muscled but lean. He is always smartly dressed, clean and neat – even in his work gear. All year, his skin is bronzed from working outdoors. He is gentle and genial and a little bit shy. He laughs a lot – tilts his head back and laughs like he really means it. He marries late but nobody knows why.

He would tell you about that week when you stayed with him and his new wife in their very new company house with everything just-so. Tell you about the afternoon, when he found you in his beautiful, symmetrical veggie garden. Dwarfed by a lush wall of runner beans, you wandered, tasting peas straight from the pod, and he just laughed and taught you about poisonous insecticides.

His wife is younger than him, a glamorous former beauty queen, a hairdresser with a perfect beehive. She trims your fringe and makes you watery orange cordial and home-baked chocolate slice, with coconut scattered on the fudgy icing.

They have a new black and orange three-seater vinyl suite and a big new television on stalky legs and a large metal wall clock – a wedding present, a sunburst blazing across the lounge wall.

You could watch that clock for hours.

He took you out to the beach in their big sleek Vauxhall Velox, you perched on the bench seat between them, legs swinging.

The new car is low slung, with whitewall tyres and American rock and roll fins.

It's a pretty shade of pineapple yellow, with a fierce, majestic British griffin on the bonnet. He keeps his car immaculate, inside and out.

Chrome glittering in the hot summer sun, the young guy at the clanking bowser is wide-eyed…envying some thing. Your uncle grins, gives him a wink and tells him to keep the change, mate. His wife rolls her eyes and clicks her tongue and he drives on, still smiling and whistling some pop song.

At the bach he'd hired, everything was spic and span, any creeping drifts of black sand quickly banished. The air was sweet with canary yellow lupins, jet pods popping in the sun. He'd run into the surf and splash, grinning and laughing as we squealed and lurched out of his briny reach. He'd tell you how he loved to be outside.

My uncle Paddy turned sixty and then, just before Easter, he drove his new Toyota to one of his favourite tracks in the ranges.

A good organiser with an eye for detail, he chose a quiet place and a quiet time.

It was carefully planned, neat…well executed.

No note.

No warning signs.

No griffin to protect him from his demons.

The outsider outside. He left nothing to chance, but he left us guessing.

If he were here, the stories my gay uncle might tell me.

Fat Tuesday Carnival

Sara Abend-Sims

'Fat Tuesday Parade – an invitation. Tinge your hair ends in red and gold,' Uncle Jack recites. 'Line your wrinkles in silver stardust. Bronze powder your cauliflower thighs, make them show through silk and tulle, through designer cuts and layered slits. Let your ankles sprout out of shoes – see-through plastic and studded glass, strapped with butterflies and wire, make your walking a balancing act.' Jack chuckles. 'I memorized it. Nice, hey?' He looks at me, apologetic. I'm not sure about the invite's poetic spell and wonder if he is kidding or has had a few, that's when he sometimes spits poetics. Has he?

'A pre-Lenten carnival, it said.' Jack's voice is clear, a smile tinges the corner of his mouth. 'I wasn't in the mood but the wording, you should admit, was quite something.'

'Yes,' I nod.

'So, I put on some garb, grabbed the note I was in the middle of writing and went out. It was a night in town where others and me, ME,' he points at his chest, 'strutted our stuff and delighted the cheering crowds.'

We are by the River Torrens, the afternoon sun is soft and shadows are growing long. I watch ducks cut the green film of algae and water, and wonder about their health. I steal a side-glance at the man by my side, and wonder about his health, then look down at the path, at his heavy boots and stylish jeans, noting to myself that he is steady on his feet. Boozing isn't part of it then. Jack's hands are busy lighting a cigarette now, and he knows to blow the smoke away from me. I look up and his eyes are dreamy, silver curls soften his brow and note his lips alternating between the tight O of sucking and the utterances of words.

'I hesitated,' he continues, 'I was in half a mind to get away from the noise, from the smell of sweat and product, but someone pushed me up and followed me to a spot on the float, where we were alongside short ones who have shrunk to nothing, and tall ones, who stretched too high. A float of all sorts celebrating together, throwing caution to the wind in this Mad Gay-Grey-Pride-Parade.'

The smoke doesn't smudge his bearing, doesn't dull the spark in his eyes. He has more talking to do and I listen to the tale of this certain night.

'Grey, gay, grey,' Jack says. 'I heard the yelling in rap, with jazz staccato drums, in sync with loudspeakers' call. I even tried some dance steps, imagine me dancing, also attempted some singing, ha, ha.' I look at him and wonder, unable to recall hearing him sing, even tapping his foot to rhythm has never been his style.

'Blow your kisses, dam-da-dam,' Jack raises his voice. 'The man next to me shouted, "Our time to shine is now, now, now; gay and proud, dam da-dam. Proud and grey, now, now, now. Blow your kisses, dam da-dam …"'

'Riding high on the night,' Jack says, his voice barely

audible now, 'I pulled the note that I grabbed on my way out.' A long pause follows this comment, before he takes a deep breath and whispers, 'My suicide note.'

He glances at me, kind of shy, saying, 'I pulled the note out of my pocket, scrunched it tight before straightening it again, and instead of reading what I'd nearly finished writing, I ripped it into fine confetti.' Jack's breathing is hurried, filled with fresh air and cigarette smoke. There's no reek of beer or whisky, just smoke laced with the faint smell of garlic. A suicide note!

'My torn words mingled with the noise, with the glitz and glamour,' Jack says. 'I watched my confetti riding the breeze and dropping to the ground, landing on fancy hairdos and trampled on by stiletto shoes or bare feet. White. Torn. Powerless. A discarded part of life, not death.'

'Oh, Jack,' I say, and kick a fallen branch. It lands by new growth shooting up from a fallen eucalypt. The movement and thud startle rainbow lorikeets. They swoop above us, screeching, their colour and noise a celebration of life.

'A bottle at hand and strutting my stuff. What a night.' Uncle Jack's hands are cupped on both sides of his mouth, as he trumpets, 'Welcome to life!'

'When back home, I had to jot this down,' Henry writes. 'Had to. I reread what I'd written, weighed words and changed some, making sure that I've done justice to Uncle Jack's turmoil and poetic gush.'

Henry rests his head in his hands and shuts his eyes, attempting to digest it all. When ready, he pulls out an old family photo where a young Jack and his wife are smiling like everybody else.

'And I wonder,' Henry keys in letters and words, 'if Jack was smiling like everybody else, if Jack had already known, and does it matter that I, Henry, understand, or is it enough that I was with him, that I've heard, that I've listened?'

Spaced

Steve Carr

The train rocked gently as the clacking of the wheels sounded through the dining car. Holding a glass of red wine a few inches from his nostrils, inhaling the rich bouquet, Uncle Morty stared out the window at a plain of yellow prairie grass under a twilight sky streaked with gold and purple.

"Do you remember Barry?" he asked.

Yes, I remembered Barry, but not well. He was Uncle Morty's boyfriend twenty years ago, when Uncle Morty was twenty-six and I was six. Uncle Morty brought Barry to our house on a few occasions for dinner or to play cards with my parents. I recalled how different he was from Uncle Morty. Barry was rugged, the outdoors type, with broad shoulders and a boisterous laugh. When he first saw me during each visit he would rub my head and call me Champ.

Uncle Morty was quiet, genteel, and not the least bit outdoorsy.

"Wasn't he the one with a red, white and blue U.S. Marines insignia tattooed on his bicep?" I asked. That's the kind of thing that impresses a six-year-old.

Uncle Morty sighed loudly. "Yes, that was him." He took a sip of the wine as he gazed at the prairie slowly blanketed by night.

I gulped down the last of my iced tea and looked around the car. Only Uncle Morty and I were still sitting at a table. The bartender was washing glasses behind the bar.

"Did I ever tell you what happened to Barry?" he asked, and then took another sip of wine.

I searched my memory and couldn't remember ever hearing what had become of Barry, but Uncle Morty had always had a steady flow of boyfriends who came and went without much explanation as to what happened to them.

Uncle Morty leaned his forehead against the glass. "I loved Barry more than I've ever loved anyone," he said mournfully. "I'm sure we'd still be together if that frightful night hadn't occurred."

I've never been much of a drinker but I suddenly wanted something strong, like straight whiskey. Uncle Morty was my mother's only brother and I grew up with him always around. By experience, I knew when he was about to start to blubber. Uncle Morty was given to crying with little provocation.

"What frightful night?" I asked, hesitantly.

He lifted his head and downed the last of the wine. Tears were rolling down his cheeks. He refilled his glass from the bottle left at the table during dinner. "See those rock formations on the horizon?" he asked.

"Yes," I answered. I had been looking at them for some time. They rose up from the horizon like jagged teeth. My mother's voice echoed in my brain: "Take the train trip west with your uncle. You know how afraid he is of flying and he would appreciate your company. Besides, you'll enjoy the scenery."

Uncle Morty chugged down half of the glass of wine. "Barry loved to go camping," he said. "To please him I bought everything a camper needs and we camped in forests, on beaches, on mountains, and then we went to the Badlands National Park." He bit into his lower lip as he choked back a sob. "We were going to spend a week there. In the first few days we saw buffalo, prairie dogs, fox, and all kinds of birds. We hiked all over the park, taking pictures and enjoying the scenery. Not once did I let on that I craved the comfort of a nice hotel room and room service." His hands shook as he drank the rest of the wine in his glass and then refilled it.

I took an ice cube from my glass and plopped it into my mouth.

"On the fourth day," he continued, "Barry wanted to hike to the top of a formation and wait there until night so that we could be closer to the stars at nightfall. It sounded wonderfully romantic and I could never refuse him anything he wanted anyway, so we waited until late afternoon and climbed to the top of a formation. We spread a blanket, stretched out on it, and waited for night." He stopped and took a long drink of his wine.

I looked towards the window. The darkness of night had turned it into a mirror. My reflection stared back at me. "Then what happened?" I asked.

He took a napkin from the table and blew his nose. "At some point we both fell asleep. We were awoken at the same time by a high-pitched humming coming from directly above us. I grabbed Barry's hand when I saw a saucer-shaped spaceship hovering overhead."

"'Don't be afraid, darling, I'll protect you,'" Barry said to me.

"Barry let loose of my hand and stood up. In that instance an opening appeared in the bottom of the ship. Then a beam of light shot out from the opening and enveloped Barry. The beam lifted him into the air, pulled him into the ship, and then the ship flew off and disappeared in space."

I crunched down hard on the ice, breaking it into pieces. "And you never saw him again?"

Uncle Morty poured the last of the wine into his glass. "It's for the best that I haven't," he said. "If he were to leave me again in any other way it would be quite anticlimactic, don't you think?"

He took a sip of his wine.

Your Grandmother, the Fag Hag

Matt Potter

"It's a *hot* summer night, Digby. Those parks would be *hopping*," your grandmother said, leaning against the kitchen bench dressed in a green chiffon caftan, red feathers ringing the cuffs. "You've got to get out there and give it a go!"

"You look like a Christmas tree after an earthquake," I said. I wiped the sink clean with a sponge and placed the sponge back behind the tap.

"You need to get out more," she continued, pursing her lips and aiming a plume of cigarette smoke at the ceiling. "And this hot weather is *perfect* for a night-time frolic ..."

I filled her glass from the flask she always carries. It didn't shut her up.

"... get your rocks off ..."

Normally Grandma spent Tuesday night sewing her latest clubbing outfit, while I'd be at my place watching television doing my needlepoint.

She gulped her vodka. "There are so many *desperate* and *lonely* men." Her voice cracked. "I don't *understand* you." She swayed as she spoke.

I glared at the clock.

"You're too *scared* to get out and experience *Life*."

Then she smacked her glass down on the benchtop and flicked ash into the sink.

Headlights bumped across potholes as I drove into the park. Cars lay in shadow.

"You'll *thank* me when you're resting your head on some gym queen's *chest*," Grandma slurred from the passenger seat.

"In a public toilet?!"

She looked through hooded eyes. "You really don't know how this works, do you?"

The road puttered to a dead end. I pulled the car over into the shadows.

"*No one* can see you here!" Grandma spat. "*No one* will go where they can't see anything. That's how you get *bashed!*"

Wrenching the car back into gear, I pulled out onto the road with a swirl of dust. There was a spot five cars ahead. I pulled in and slammed the brakes.

Grandma's head bounced against the headrest. "With all this *testosterone* you're displaying, you really *must* need a fuck!"

Cars drifted in.

Drifted out.

Hung around.

It was so quiet, you could hear a used condom drop.

Grandma wound down the window and lit a cigarette. She blew the smoke out through the window. It blew back in.

"This is very boring," I coughed, flapping my hands about to disperse her smoke.

"*Something* will happen," Grandma replied, dragging on her cigarette through red feathers. "It *always* does."

"In my seventeen years since coming out," I said, "I have never prowled around public parks and snuck into public toilets."

Twenty seconds later, a man, possibly in his early twenties (I couldn't quite tell through the darkness) stepped out of his car. I watched his pneumatic bottom charge across the grass towards the toilet block.

Then at least five (maybe more) men stepped out of their cars and converged in hot pursuit.

"He's not my type," I said.

"He looks *great*. Very hot and cute and *throbbing*."

"You can tell in the dark without your glasses?"

She clamped her mouth shut.

Then threw her cigarette butt through the window. Opening the door, she stepped out and ground it into the dirt with her heel.

"We'll get arrested for littering."

She looked across the car roof and surveyed the view.

Then breaking into a swift stride, she charged towards the toilet block. Flashes of chiffon disappeared into the darkness.

"Where are you going?!" I rasped through the driver's window.

*

I held my breath as I walked into the toilet block, my soles gritty on the cement floor.

How many bashers lay in wait?

I poked my head around a low wall.

No one stood waiting.

One cubicle covered with swirls of toilet paper.

Then in the other cubicle ...

eyes adjusted to the darkness ...

a fumbling man ...

of about ninety ...

brandishing a red and sorry-looking penis. He smiled sheepishly and tightened his wizened grip.

"Hi," I said. "I'm looking for my mother."

His panting and my feet on the floor were the only sounds as I ran out of the toilet block.

A path snuck off to the left into a clump of trees.

"Psssst! They're over here."

Red feathers flashed as hands pulled me down to a crouch. I nested behind a large pine tree as needles pricked my face.

"He headed for *the bushes* instead," your grandmother said. Her eyes glistened in the pale moonlight. "It's all *happening* up that path. You can see through that *gap*."

I looked through the gap between the foliage. A man sauntered towards us. Short mousy hair. Blue T-shirt. Jeans.

Closer, I saw sculpted features. Broad shoulders. Erect nipples under his t-shirt.

Grandma waved her hands at me to follow him. "He's got a *big* dick."

My eyes widened.

"I've *seen* it. He's a *stripper*."

I shifted balance. My knees were hurting from the crouching.

"He's coming *back*," she said, and pushed me, sending me sprawling. Right into his path.

He pulled up just as he was about to step on my fingers.

White running shoes. I looked up. Faded denim. Then lunchy bulge and a tight t-shirt.

He held out his hand and pulled me to my feet, his grip manly but his touch gentle.

I whispered "thank you" as I gazed into the eyes of an Adonis. And as I had my very first out-of-body experience, I heard the lamest line in the world tumble from my lips: "Do you come here often?"

The groan from the cover of the trees was heard for miles.

He smiled a cover boy smile.

Leaves rustled. A breeze cooled my forehead. Something grabbed my ankle and tugged. I shook my foot, then realised it was your grandmother.

"Excuse me," I spluttered, and ducked behind the pine tree again.

"Make some *small* talk," she hissed.

She pushed me back onto the path. In the distance the Adonis was now talking to another man.

"Don't miss your *chance*," she hissed again.

I heard noises from the direction of the toilet block. The old man came walking towards me, a leer plastered across his face.

My forehead prickled with heat. My tongue was fat and furry.

I looked down at the bitumen path. Up into the trees. Beyond the trees and up into the starry sky.

The leer lurched closer.

Should I retreat behind the pine tree again?

"Go *after* him!"

The Adonis stood in the distance but nowhere looked safe.

Old man feet scuffing on the path grew closer.

I turned and met his stare.

There was lust in his rheumy eyes.

He grabbed his crotch.

I ducked behind the tree and bobbed down out of sight.

Then I smelt stale breath hot on my face as he ducked behind the tree too.

He winked.

"I'll do both you and your mother for fifty bucks," he said.

He smacked his lips.

Your grandmother's voice cut through the night air. "I'll give you twenty if you fuck *off.*"

He stuck out his hand.

Your grandmother pulled a red twenty-dollar bill from her bra and slapped it into his open palm.

He stuffed the note in his pocket.

Then the world's oldest hustler shuffled off into the darkness.

"So how did the evening turn out?" I ask.

"The Adonis turned out to be a *part-time* stripper and a *full-time* undercover cop."

"Oh," I say.

"Who turned out to be a really great guy *anyway*, and very good at needlepoint, *too*."

"Oh," I say again.

"And it was through him I met your Uncle Steve."

"Oh."

"And that's why your grandmother received an OAM for services to the gay community. Because she was always willing to give anything a *go*."

A Chance Encounter

Carl Chapman

My uncle related this story about a friend of his named Willie, but with each telling of one of his *stories*, I think he was telling me a little more about himself. Here's how his story went…

Willie couldn't keep his eyes away from Terry's screensaver on his computer: a series of photos of muscular nude men in erotic poses, most of whom had penises the size of which he only dreamed of. He'd never have the nerve to freely show anything like that on his computer at home.

Willie repositioned himself in his easy chair as he studied Terry, while Terry made the two of them a cup of tea. They had run into each other at a nearby bar. He had no idea Terry lived so close to him. They'd worked together on a production of *Bus Stop*. He was the director and Terry played Bo, the hot-looking mean-tempered cowboy, which he had to admit was typecasting when it came to Terry.

He couldn't help but glance at the well-made king size bed. Would the two of them end up there soon? Part of him hoped so and part of him was terrified they would. If so, this was going to be his first time being with a man. Now he knew what virgins must feel like on their wedding night. A combination of excitement and dread.

Would it go well? Would they be compatible? Would he freak out?

Terry set the cup of tea in front of him, then sat down in the chair opposite him, looking at the screensaver and smirking.

"What do you think?" he asked.

"Very nice."

"Does it turn you on?"

"Yes." Willie responded without first editing his answer.

"Good."

Willie glanced at the bed again. Maybe this isn't a good idea, he thought. Maybe I should find a way to get out of here before this goes too far.

Terry stood and moved toward him, his bathrobe opening just enough to show that he had nothing on, and to show just what he had to offer should they go all the way. Willie couldn't help but be impressed. The photos on the screen saver had a lot in common with Terry's physique.

Willie got excited by the quick reveal. God, was this really happening? Was he really going to finally have sex with a man? He'd considered it many times but always pulled away from the thought when it became too overwhelming, like now.

The situation brought him back to a time in high school when he was encouraged by the wrestling coach to join the team because they needed someone in his weight class. He'd gone with the coach to the locker room to be weighed and while in there watched as another player was being weighed. He was a well-built beautifully tanned senior who, and there was no other way to explain it, had the body of Adonis. Willie nearly freaked when they asked this perfect specimen of a young man to take off his jock strap and stand on the scale. The senior quickly removed his near-nothing covering and stood naked on the scale in all his glory. The arousal Willie felt upon viewing his naked body was almost immediate, so much so that he dreaded possibly disrobing because it would reveal just how excited the sight of the young man made him. Why did they have him take off his jock strap? How much could a thing like that weigh? Was it necessary to get completely naked? His arousal was immediate and quite real. It took everything in him to control his body while he was weighed. After the experience in the locker room he decided maybe wrestling wasn't for him after all.

Terry moved in close behind Willie as he sat, and started rubbing his shoulders.

Relax. Nothing's going to happen that you don't want to happen, Willie assured himself.

But that's what worried Willie: he did want it to happen. However, he knew that he couldn't always trust his judgement. His impulses had caused him trouble numerous times before and brought about one not so friendly divorce.

Willie could feel himself aroused as he felt Terry's hard cock rubbing against the back of his shoulders.

After a moment Terry's robe dropped down by his feet and he knew Terry was standing completely nude behind him. All he had to do was turn around. And in a sudden movement he had that opportunity as Terry pulled on his shoulder to turn him around, then with both hands pushed him to his knees, so that he was staring straight at Terry's erect manhood inches from his lips. Willie opened wide and swallowed all of him. It was everything he imagined it would be. It was glorious. He took all of him into his mouth and fed on him like a child might its first chance at a mother's nipple. Yes, it had taken a long time to get to this moment but now that it was here, Willie knew he'd found what he'd been destined to discover.

He tugged Terry down to the floor and tasted him, over and over, rubbing his body all over his and tearing away his own clothes as they fell into a heated pairing that went on for what seemed to be hours. They never even made it to the bed. Willie had found what he'd always been searching for, and now that he'd found it, he was never going to let it go.

Now, I don't know if that story was about my uncle or not, but it turned me on so much that it made me question my own sexuality.

The Man Who Came to Stay

Ruth Z. Deming

It was the month of June, a rainy Saturday morning. Mom and Dad told us Uncle Peter would be arriving any moment, driven by the airport limousine. The word "gay" was used for the first time in our presence. In my parents' bedroom I asked Daddy what the word meant. "Sex with other men," was his short reply. I asked Daddy if he had ever had sex with other men. "Certainly not," he said in an angry voice.

Our dead Grandpa Charlie had once lived with us. He was a physician and a teacher. In the den were shelves of his old textbooks. When curiosity overtook me, I would leaf through the pages and view unforgettable images. Babies who were neither girls nor boys. Twins whose heads were attached. The worst, however, was a close-up of a person with elephantiasis in an African desert. The caption read, "Transmitted by a worm caused by mosquitos."

Was my gay uncle like any of those people?

At night, I lay awake in terror.

Mom had a table of snacks ready for Uncle Peter and the rest of us. Deviled eggs, tiny tuna fish on rye sandwiches, and kippered herring on Melba toast.

How I loved when we had company.

We heard a screeching of brakes in the front yard. Was he here? We all rushed to the front door and saw a man in a straw hat emerge, smiling, from the limousine. In his hands, which were quite red, he carried two large bags.

"Why, Uncle Peter," said Mom, kissing him on the cheek. "We are so happy to see you. Come in, come in."

He wiped his wet feet on the 'Welcome to our Home' mat, removed his straw hat and shook it in the air, dispersing little droplets.

As we walked inside, the whistle of the tea kettle rang merrily.

"Everything but a roaring fire," laughed our uncle.

We all sat around the dining room table. Mom poured the tea into grown-up cups and saucers. Birds of all kinds graced the cups; they seemed ready to fly off to South America, Seattle, or Los Angeles, where our uncle lived.

"Tell us, Peter," said Daddy, "What is new on the actors circuit? Have you gotten any new parts? We knew you were in *The Rockford Files* and *Hawaii Five-O*."

"Oh," said Uncle, who put down his steaming tea and ran his palms through his wet black hair.

Was it dyed like the men on television, I wondered.

"I'm afraid the parts have all dried up," answered Uncle Peter. "I tested for Bob Fosse's movie *All That Jazz*, where I'd play one of the board of directors, but I was sent home. Bad luck over and over again."

"Don't worry, Uncle Peter," I said staring at his long fingernails, which needed a good trimming, "You can stay here."

Silence filled the room.

"If you don't mind," said Uncle Peter, "may I go to my room and take a nap?"

He left his suitcases at the table.

Upstairs he trudged. At the top of the stairs he called, "I've got presents for everyone. Let me snooze for ten minutes and then we'll chat."

As everyone knows, there are two kinds of people: ones who give great gifts and others who are simply clueless.

Loud snores like train whistles bounced out of his room.

Soon we heard a loud yawn and the proclamation, "I am awake, my darlings."

We repaired back to the dining room table. Outside the rain had stopped and the clouds drifted like huge bundles of icing on a wedding cake.

Onto the table Uncle Peter deposited books and calendars for everyone.

We learned a lot about our uncle.

He had almost married, he said, but was "afraid of commitment."

He was godfather to the children of a number of celebrities, including Mario Puzo from *The Godfather*, Eugene Roche from *Slaughterhouse-Five* and Cliff Robertson from *The Great Northfield Minnesota Raid*.

"Daddy," I asked from the dining room table, where we all helped ourselves to a bowl of salted peanuts. "Can you take me to see some of those movies?"

"Someday," he said, "but six-year-olds are too young…"

Uncle Peter jumped in. "Oh, you would be shocked, little lady, to find a dead horse's head under the covers," he said.

I screamed and ran out of the room.

I wasn't so sure I wanted him to stay after that.

When You Go Walking with Your Uncle

Nod Ghosh

My Uncle Jayash is six months younger than me. Back home, I would be his first cousin once removed. But here in the bosom of our Indian family, I'm his nephew, or bhagne. The network of aunts, uncles, great grandparents and siblings who make up our extended family are fastidious in the way they name each other. There are Jhetus and Sejos. Bowdis and Mejos. No one is addressed by their actual name unless they fall lower in a defined hierarchy, or if they've done something wrong. My Kakima is someone else's Didi, and my Didi, if I had one, would be Jayash's niece.

It's confusing.

Our family tree is like spaghetti. Or more like the vermicelli pudding our mutual ancestor makes. Boroma is my great grandmother and Jayash's maternal grandmother. She regularly cooks vermicelli and other *mishti*, even though she's a hundred years old. She's half my height and needs a stool to reach the pot high on the stove, where she stirs her concoction with agitated movements, and drops in brown lumps of jaggery.

Jayash addresses Boroma as Didima. Her real name is Parvati, but no one is allowed to call her that.

It does my fucking head in.

"Come on, Navin," Jayash says. "Let's go."

His mother, Great Aunt Moushumi or Mouma as I have been trained to call her, furrows her brow.

"What?" my uncle says. He tucks a wad of rupees from a tin on the shelf into the pocket of his jeans, and we're out of there. My flight only touched down a few hours ago, and I'm desperate for sleep.

Sleep can wait.

"So how's med school, Navin?" Jayash is allowed to call me by my first name even though I'm the elder. He uses it whenever he can, as if relishing the opportunity. He has that on me, through being my mother's youngest brother. And by brother, I mean first cousin, but over here, there is no difference.

"I'm thinking of dropping out," I say, flicking a halo of flies off my face. There's a guy selling lychees on the side of the road. He only has one eye.

"Oh?" Jayash fills a bag and breaks off from our conversation to haggle with the one-eyed fruit-seller. I find the man's sunken socket disturbing, but he's not all that's troubling me.

It's not just dissection that bothers me at Uni, though the memory of embalmed flesh yielding under my scalpel turns my stomach. There's so much more I am uncertain about.

"Medicine's not my thing," I tell Jayash, piercing a lychee's hard shell to reach soft flesh inside. The flavour is indescribable. The tinned fruit I buy in Dunedin, when craving something exotic, is aluminium to this silver fragrance.

A memory of feeding Caroline lychees flickers through my mind. I remember being lost in the ecstasy of our lovemaking, lost in the rhythm of our heartbeats, being lost in the flavour of soft white fruit. Sharing. Biting. Sucking.

I grab two more pieces from the bag and look for somewhere to put the first pip. Jayash catapults his into the gutter. "I want to do something different," I tell him.

"Well, what?" Is that a patronising tone? Or is it concern?

"That's the thing," I say. "I have no idea."

"Lucky you have choices," he says.

The last time I was here, we were eleven. Jayash and I would skip along the footpath near Mouma's house, both burning with the flame of possibility and promise, so determined to change the world. So certain we could. Whenever we talked about choices, we thought we had it all.

"That's the thing," I say after a while, "I'm not sure I ever did have a free choice. Some things are predetermined, but they're not always right."

"There was once a prince," Jayash holds up a finger, "who knew little about choice." He continues as if I haven't spoken. I surreptitiously drop shiny pips and their red husks into the gutter. "He was the son of a powerful Raja." He's using his *storytelling* voice. It's time for me to listen, not speak. A strong scent of sandalwood hits the air. We're passing stalls selling incense and figurines of deities. An emaciated woman displays woven baskets and straw fans on a tattered blanket.

"When it was time to marry, his father introduced him to the most accomplished women in the land," Jayash continues. "They danced for the prince. He heard them play musical instruments, recite poetry." Jayash marches forward with purpose as he speaks. Though my legs are longer than his, I find it hard to keep up. It's only then that I realise I have no clue where we're going. "There were astronomers and priestesses. Some were mathematicians."

I wonder if the 'prince' is about to be presented with a carpenter's wife. I hope Jayash will break into laughter, and we'll joke about how we'd listened to his *Blood on the Tracks* cassette a thousand times when we were eleven, until Mouma's tape recorder chewed it up and turned it into vermicelli mishti.

But he isn't. He doesn't.

"The prince refused every single one," he continues. "Eventually the Raja asked his son, 'whom *do* you want as your bride?'"

There's a moment of silence, before Jayash continues in a small voice.

"And the prince replied, 'It's not a bride I want.'" He is silent.

"What happened next?" I ask.

"His father banished him from the kingdom." Jayash stops walking, the half-empty bag of lychees slack in his hand.

I stop too, uncertain what to say or do.

"We're here," he says.

"Where?" I ask.

A man opens the door and lets us in.

"This is Navin," Jayash says, and introduces Kishon to me.

There's something about the way this guy Kishon looks at Jayash. I've seen that look before. It makes me think of Caroline licking juice from my fingers. I follow him in.

We share the remaining lychees.

Kiss

Edward O'Dwyer

My uncle told me the true story of his wedding day so I could use it to contribute to an anthology of stories told by gay uncles. He insists, however, that I mention he's single and available again, and makes a mean Appletini.

The occasion had been a triumph so far. All the guests were turned out in their finest, and all of them were in such high spirits, thrilled for the happy couple.

"I now pronounce you man and wife," announced the justice of the peace.

"Ah, actually, don't you mean pronounce us man and man?" the groom quickly interjected. That is, the one who wasn't wearing the big white dress and the veil.

"Oh, am, yes, of course I do," the justice of the peace recovered, at last taking notice of the thick black hair on the knuckles clenched around the bouquet. "You may now kiss the, am... kiss the... am..."

"The bride," the groom growled, letting out a weary sigh, unable to work out just what was so difficult about it all.

Contributors

RubinA

RubinA is an Australian-based actor and writer of Indian origin. She has been a hobby-poet for some time, and professionally has been involved in the media industry in various capacities for over ten years. Her aim is to become a successful published author. She especially loves writing for children.

Alex Reece Abbott

A finalist in flash prizes including the Bridport, Reflex, Maria Edgeworth, Bath, Fish, Bath Novella-in-Flash and Ad Hoc Fiction, Alex's work features in *Bonsai: Best Small Stories* from *Aotearoa New Zealand*, *Pure Slush*, *Bath* and *NFFD* anthologies, *Splonk*, *Fictive Dream*, *Flash Frontier*, *Pulp Literature*, *Hypertext*, *Spelk* and *The Nottingham Review* among others. She is a Kathy Fish Fellowship and Penguin Random House WriteNow novel finalist, an Irish Novel Fair winner and multiple Best Microfictions nominee.

Sara Abend-Sims

Sara Abend-Sims was born in Poland and grew up in Israel. She lived in London for a short while and is now living in Adelaide, Australia. She is a University of SA graduate who has worked as community support, lecturer and counsellor. Sara has travelled, written, painted and exhibited her art in Australia and overseas. In the last decade she has been using words instead of brushes, capturing moments and attempting to make sense of her own experience as well as others. She is the recipient of two community first prize literary awards – 2009 and 2015 – and her stories and poetry have been published in anthologies, journals and online in Australia and overseas.

Henry Bladon

Henry Bladon is based in Somerset in the UK. He is a writer of short fiction and poetry and teaches creative writing for therapeutic purposes. He has degrees in psychology and mental health policy, and a PhD in literature and creative writing. He frequently writes commentary about mental health issues and his literary work can be seen in *O:JA&L*, *Fewer than 500*, *FlashFrontier*, *The Ekphrastic Review*, and *Spillwords Press*, among other places.

Steve Bogdaniec

Steve Bogdaniec is a writer and teacher, currently teaching at Wright College, Chicago. Steve has had poetry and short fiction published in numerous journals, most recently in *Eclectica Magazine*, *Silver Birch Press*, and *Jellyfish Review*. His work can also be found in the *Nancy Drew Anthology: Writing & Art Inspired by Everyone's Favorite Female Sleuth.* Check out stevebogdaniec.com for links to published work and updates on new stuff.

Steve Carr

Steve Carr, who lives in Richmond, Virginia, has had over 300 short stories published internationally in print and online magazines, literary journals and anthologies since June 2016. Four collections of his short stories, *Sand, Rain, Heat,* and *The Tales of Talker Knock,* have been published. His plays have been produced in several states in the U.S. and he has been nominated for a Pushcart Prize twice.

Helen Chambers

Helen Chambers is a short story and flash fiction writer from North East Essex, UK, who dreams up ideas whilst out walking by the river. She has an MA in Creative Writing from the University of Essex and she won the Fish Short Story prize in 2018. Helen has several publications, many of which you can read on her blog: https://helenchamberswriter.wordpress.com.

Carl Chapman

Carl Chapman has a M.A. in English from UMKC and a B.F.A. in Speech and Theatre from Avila University. His recognized stage plays include *Caught Between Two Worlds,* published by Dramatic Publishing, and *Folktales for Fun,* published by Pioneer Drama Service, Inc. Carl's stage play *Cleansing Acts* recently placed in the 2015 William Faulkner Literary Competition, while a production of the play itself premiered at the 2013 LaBute New Theatre Festival in St. Louis, Missouri by the St. Louis Actors' Studio, and was named winner of the Riverfront Times newspaper's 'Best of 2013 Stage Plays'.

Chuka Susan Chesney

Chuka Susan Chesney's mother Helen Watkins Farson grew up in Depression-era Oklahoma, one of eight children deserted by their physician father. Many of the members of the family moved to Southern California in the late 1940s. Helen met Chesney's father Kenneth at the local Presbyterian church. Ken's family owned a printing business and talked endlessly about books and movies and played lots of Scrabble. Chesney grew up in a world of literature and graphics. She is a graduate of Art Center College of Design.

Carolyn Cordon

Cordon Cordon is a writer, poet, blogger and is the Editor of the *Mallala Crossroad Chronicle*. She regularly speaks on PBAFM, a Public Radio station for Salisbury and areas close by. Community is her 'big thing', particularly when it gives chances for sharing words, spoken, and written. She is also the President and Competition Secretary for Adelaide Plains Poets, a writing group that meets weekly in Gawler. This group puts on the Gawler and Adelaide Plains Festival of Words. Sometimes she actually writes some more of her novel she's been working on for what seems like years ...

Ruth Z. Deming

Ruth Z. Deming writes from her home in Willow Grove, PA, a suburb of Philadelphia in the good ole USA. Most mornings she eats breakfast while watching a film noir on YouTube. A psychotherapist, she runs New Directions, a support group for people with depression, bipolar disorder and their loved ones. View www.newdirectionssupport.org. She and about 12 other poets, short story writers and novelists attend The Beehive, an every Saturday writing group where gentle feedback is offered. Her blog is www.ruthzdeming.blogspot.com. She has been published in *Pure Slush*, *Mad Swirl*, *Literary Yard* and *Scarlet Leaf Publishing*.

EG Downs

EG Downs is a full time restaurant manager and sporadic writer living in Brooklyn, New York, but originally from the Deep South. Her work has appeared in print but mostly online. She loves butter, but not *that* much.

Tom Fegan

Tom Fegan was raised working in his family's restaurant Burger & Shake in Fort Worth, Texas. After graduation from college he spent several years in the steel industry. Contentedly divorced and employed as a security professional, he works towards growth in his writing career.

Nod Ghosh

Nod Ghosh lives in Christchurch, New Zealand, and completed a creative writing course at the Hagley Writers' Institute. Nod's flash fiction, short stories and poems have appeared in the New Zealand publications, *JAAM*, *Landfall*, *North and South Magazine*, *Takahē*, *Headland* and *Flash Frontier*. Nod's work also appears in *London Grip*, *Connotation Press*, *Blue Fifth Review*, *The Citron Review*, *Spelk Fiction*, *The Airgonaut*, *Brilliant Flash Fiction*, *Fictive Dream*, *Peacock Journal*, *MiNDFOOD*, *Pure Slush* and other international publications. Nod's novella-in-flash *The Crazed Wind* was published by Truth Serum Press in July 2018.

Jan Haag

Jan Haag teaches journalism and creative writing at Sacramento City College in Sacramento, California, and on weekends facilitates community writing groups to remind people that their voices are worthy of the page. She is finishing her second novel and is the author of a poetry collection, *Companion Spirit*, published by Amherst Writers & Artists Press. Her website is janishaag.com.

Chris Hall

Chris Hall lives in Adelaide, South Australia and has worked for well over 30 years as a nurse, predominantly in mental health, where he learned that nothing can afflict you more than your own intrusive thoughts. So, he writes as a diversion. He enjoys telling stories because they explain where you've been, but they don't have to dictate where you're going. It's only after we realise we have drifted astray that we resolve to find ourselves. Chris has been previously published in *Pride Vol. 7*, part of Pure Slush's 7 Deadly Sins series.

Alisdair Hodgson

Alisdair Hodgson is a writer, poet, freelance editor and joint editor-in-chief at Bandit Fiction. His literary interests tend towards minimalism, hysterical realism, transgression and anything postmodern, and his poetry and prose can be found in a variety of magazines, journals and anthologies. He also takes a keen interest in animal rights and regularly frequents Twitter @Youthanised.

Eddy Knight

Eddy Knight was born and raised in Britain's West Country, arriving in South Australia in 1990. As an actor or director he has worked with Howard Barker's The Wrestling School, both in the U.K. and for the Adelaide 2000 Festival, the Bell Shakespeare Company, Red Stitch Actors' Theatre, State Theatre of South Australia, Brink, and many of Adelaide's semi-professional companies. He recently gained a PhD in Creative Writing, has had plays produced locally and in New Zealand, and short stories published in Pure Slush's 7 Deadly Sins anthologies, and on the Tablo.io website.

Lance Manion

Lance Manion has released eight collections of humorous/odd short stories, has been published in more than fifty literary publications and has contributed stories to a dozen anthologies. His most recent book, *neXt*, is a short story collection, and you can find additional info on his website where he blogs regularly: https://www.lancemanion.com/.

Colleen Moyne

Colleen Moyne is a published freelance writer living in the lovely riverside town of Mannum in South Australia. She has won awards for her poetry and has had poems and short stories published in thirteen different anthologies. Her collection *Time Like Coins* was published in early 2019. Learn more about Colleen's work by visiting www.colleenmoyne.com.

Edward O'Dwyer

Edward O'Dwyer's poetry collections *The Rain on Cruise's Street* and *Bad News, Good News, Bad News* (Salmon Poetry, 2014 and 2017) have drawn comparisons with Raymond Carver and Billy Collins and been Highly Commended in the Forward Prizes. The latter contains the Michael Hartnett Festival 2018 award-winning poem, 'The Whole History of Dancing'. His third book is a dark comedy flash fiction collection, *Cheat Sheets* (Truth Serum Press, 2018), which featured on *The Lonely Crowd* journal's 'Best Books of 2018' list. *Exquisite Prisons*, his collection of poems, is due from Salmon Poetry in Spring 2020.

DeLeon W. Peacock

DeLeon W. Peacock is a published author. He resides on Saint Simons Island, Georgia USA and spends much of his time writing about his life as a gay orphan. Before DeLeon came out he was married twice and has a son and daughter. He feels very fortunate to live near the Atlantic Ocean and takes advantage of island life. He serves as president of the local Unitarian Universalist congregation and uses some of his time to raise funds for the orphanage he called home as a child.

Matt Potter

Matt Potter is the author of a travel memoir, *Hamburgers and Berliners and other courses in between*; two collections of short fiction and non-fiction, *Vestal Aversion* and *Based on True Stories*; the ESL teaching resources *all you need is ... a whiteboard, a marker and this book! Books 1 and 2*; and the novella *On the Bitch*. Also a teacher and social worker, he lives in Adelaide, South Australia where he now works in childcare, and as a publisher and editor.

Melisa Quigley

Melisa Quigley likes writing different genres and she is currently writing her first novel. In her spare time, she loves reading, cooking and doing yoga as well as spending time with her husband and two dogs. She lives in Melbourne and has had short stories, poetry and flash fiction published in several anthologies.

Michèle Saint-Yves

Michèle Saint-Yves lives in Adelaide and writes texts primarily for performance, with three full-length and three one-act plays staged since 2010 and three WIP plays selected through national competitions for staged professional readings since 2015. Michèle is completing her debut novel, supported by an Arts South Australia Emerging Writers Richard Llewellyn Deaf and Disabled Grant (2017). Michèle's had a novella shortlisted for the UK-based MsLexia Women's Novella Award 2019 and a short story published in *Southerly Journal 76.3*.

E. M. Stormo

E. M. Stormo is an editor by day, a writer by night, and a teacher and promoter of musical literacy at all times. His recent work has appeared in *The Conium Review*, *Pure Slush*, *Fresh Anthology* by Montag Press, and *Entropy Magazine*.

Susan Whitmore

Susan Whitmore currently lives in Adelaide, South Australia, with her husband, daughter, and mini-schnauzer Rufus. A writer since childhood, her stories are inspired by the world, both real and imaginary. Susan has two degrees in writing, a BA from the University of Canberra and a MPhil from the University of Queensland. Previous publications include a story in *First*, a collection of short stories published by the University of Canberra.

About Truth Serum Press

Truth Serum Press is based in Adelaide, Australia, but publishes books from authors in all parts of the English-speaking world. We were first thought of in mid-2013 but properly came into existence in mid-2014.

Like sister presses Pure Slush Books and Everytime Press, Truth Serum Press is part of the Bequem Publishing collective.

Truth Serum Press publishes novels, novellas, and short story collections. We no longer publish single author poetry anthologies.

Sometimes, when the mood strikes us, we publish multi-author anthologies, of which *Stories My Gay Uncle Told Me*, is one.

We publish fiction … and sometimes (just sometimes) we publish non-fiction.

We publish in English, and we would gladly publish in other languages if we understood them.

We like books that take us to new places, to new experiences and inside new minds and hearts.

We also like to laugh.

If you think we might like your novel or novella or short story collection, contact us at truthserumpress@live.com.au.

Visit our website at https://truthserumpress.net/.

Also from TRUTH SERUM PRESS

https://truthserumpress.net/catalogue/

 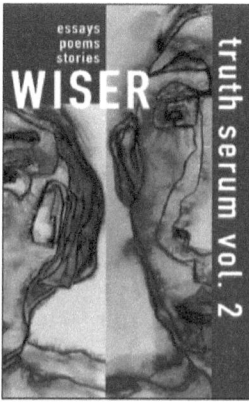 

- *The Last Free Man* by Lewis Woolston
  978-1-925536-88-1 (paperback) 978-1-925536-89-8 (eBook)
- *Wiser Truth Serum Vol. #2*
  978-1-925536-31-7 (paperback) 978-1-925536-32-4 (eBook)
- *True Truth Serum Vol. #1*
  978-1-925536-29-4 (paperback) 978-1-925536-30-0 (eBook)

 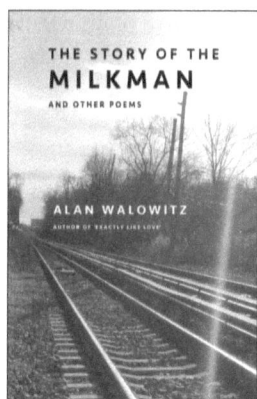 

- *Minotaur and Other Stories* by Salvatore Difalco
  978-1-925536-79-9 (paperback) 978-1-925536-80-5 (eBook)
- *The Story of the Milkman* by Alan Walowitz
  978-1-925536-76-8 (paperback) 978-1-925536-77-5 (eBook)
- *The Book of Acrostics* by John Lambremont, Sr.
  978-1-925536-52-2 (paperback) 978-1-925536-53-9 (eBook)

Also from TRUTH SERUM PRESS

https://truthserumpress.net/catalogue/

- *Square Pegs* by Rob Walker
  978-1-925536-62-1 (paperback) 978-1-925536-63-8 (eBook)
- *Cheat Sheets* by Edward O'Dwyer
  978-1-925536-60-7 (paperback) 978-1-925536-61-4 (eBook)
- *The Crazed Wind* by Nod Ghosh
  978-1-925536-58-4 (paperback) 978-1-925536-59-1 (eBook)

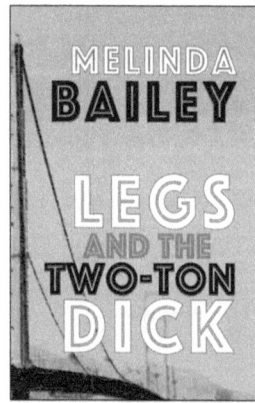  

- *Legs and the Two-Ton Dick* by Melinda Bailey
  978-1-925536-37-9 (paperback) 978-1-925536-38-6 (eBook)
- *Dollhouse Masquerade* by Samuel E. Cole
  978-1-925536-43-0 (paperback) 978-1-925536-44-7 (eBook)
- *Kiss Kiss* by Paul Beckman
  978-1-925536-21-8 (paperback) 978-1-925536-22-5 (eBook)

Also from TRUTH SERUM PRESS

https://truthserumpress.net/catalogue/

  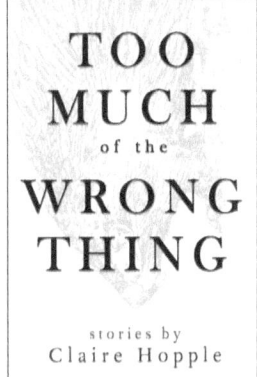

- *Inklings* by Irene Buckler
  978-1-925536-41-6 (paperback) 978-1-925536-42-3 (eBook)
- *On the Bitch* by Matt Potter
  978-1-925536-45-4 (paperback) 978-1-925536-46-1 (eBook)
- *Too Much of the Wrong Thing* by Claire Hopple
  978-1-925536-33-1 (paperback) 978-1-925536-34-8 (eBook)

- *Track Tales* by Mercedes Webb-Pullman
  978-1-925536-35-5 (paperback) 978-1-925536-36-2 (eBook)
- *Luck and Other Truths* by Richard Mark Glover
  978-1-925101-77-5 (paperback) 978-1-925536-04-1 (eBook)
- *Hello Berlin!* by Jason S. Andrews
  978-1-925536-11-9 (paperback) 978-1-925536-12-6 (eBook)

Also from TRUTH SERUM PRESS

https://truthserumpress.net/catalogue/

 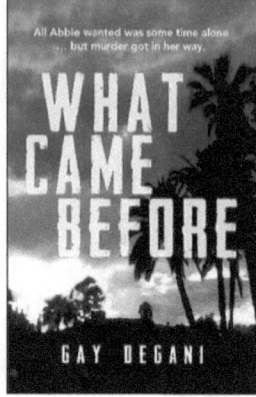 

- *Deer Michigan* by Jack C. Buck
  978-1-925536-25-6 (paperback) 978-1-925536-26-3 (eBook)
- *What Came Before* by Gay Degani
  978-1-925536-05-8 (paperback) 978-1-925536-06-5 (eBook)
- *Rain Check* by Levi Andrew Noe
  978-1-925536-09-6 (paperback) 978-1-925536-10-2 (eBook)

 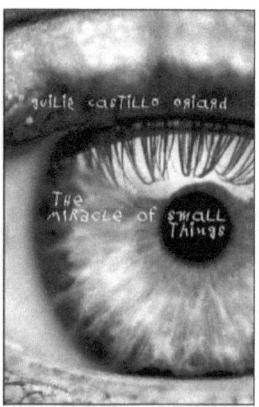 

- *Based on True Stories* by Matt Potter
  978-1-925101-75-1 (paperback) 978-1-925101-76-8 (eBook)
- *The Miracle of Small Things* by Guilie Castillo Oriard
  978-1-925101-73-7 (paperback) 978-1-925101-74-4 (eBook)
- *La Ronde* by Townsend Walker
  978-1-925101-64-5 (paperback) 978-1-925101-65-2 (eBook)

www.ingramcontent.com/pod-product-compliance
Lightning Source LLC
Chambersburg PA
CBHW050827180626
46814CB00004B/1504